Welcome to Harlequin's great new series,
created by some of our bestselling authors
from Down Under:

 THE AUSTRALIANS

Twelve tales of heated romance and adventure—
guaranteed to turn your whole world upside down!

Travel to an Outback cattle station, experience the
glamour of the Gold Coast or visit the bright lights
of Sydney where you'll meet twelve engaging young
women, all feisty and all about to face their biggest
challenge yet...falling in love.

And it will take some very special women to tame
our heroes! Strong, rugged, often infuriating and
always irresistible, they're one hundred percent prime
Australian male: hard to get close to...but even
harder to forget!

The Wonder from Down Under:
where spirited women win the hearts of
Australia's most independent men.

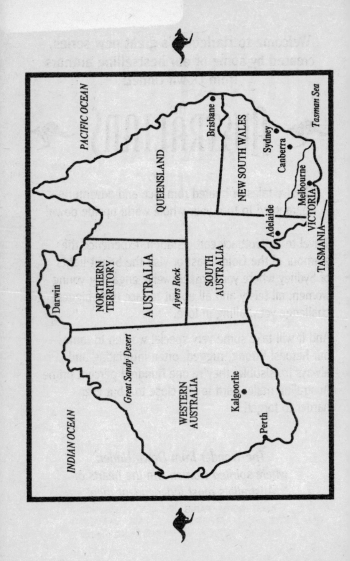

THE
AUSTRALIANS

WILDCAT
WIFE

Lindsay Armstrong

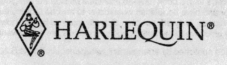

HARLEQUIN®

TORONTO • NEW YORK • LONDON
AMSTERDAM • PARIS • SYDNEY • HAMBURG
STOCKHOLM • ATHENS • TOKYO • MILAN • MADRID
PRAGUE • WARSAW • BUDAPEST • AUCKLAND

ISBN 0-373-82582-X

WILDCAT WIFE

First North American Publication 1999.

Printed in U.S.A.

Lindsay Armstrong was born in South Africa, but now lives in Australia with her New Zealand-born husband and their five children. They have lived in nearly every state of Australia and tried their hand at some unusual, for them, occupations, such as farming and horse training—all grist to the mill for a writer! Lindsay started writing romances when their youngest child began school and Lindsay was left feeling at a loose end. She is still doing it and loving it.

CHAPTER ONE

'SAFFRON, here's *another* commission—what are we going to do?' Delia Renfrew asked in wondering tones as she laid a letter in front of her boss.

Saffron Shaw pushed a hand through her cloud of russet hair, pushed away some sketches she was working on and stuck her pen behind her ear. She'd started her own interior decorating business a few years ago and called it The Crocus Shop after her unusual name—saffron being an autumn crocus, as she'd been informed by her father. And years of hard work, innovative ideas and her sense of style were now being richly rewarded so that she could barely handle the work she had.

'Who is it? Anyone we know?' she responded in an attractively husky voice that, although quite un-contrived, was as much her trademark as the crocus flowers that labelled her designs.

'No. At least, I don't know a Fraser A. Ross, do you?'

Saffron grinned and picked up the letter. 'Could he be anything but a Scot? You'd have to bet that the A stands for either Alistair, Archie, Andrew or Angus. And how pompous does it sound anyway?' She deepened her voice and puffed out her cheeks. 'Fraser *A*. Ross! I'm only surprised he hasn't added Esquire!'

'He does want you to do his whole house, though,' Delia said through her laughter.

7

'Mmm…mmm…' Saffron scanned the page. 'His *holiday* house. Mmm…on an island in the Whitsundays!'

'It's lovely up there,' Delia remarked.

'It's also a long way away, and islands are notoriously difficult spots to get to and from. No,' Saffron said with decision. 'You can write back to Mr Fraser A. Ross and tell him that I'm allergic to people who use their middle initials, that I've got the distinct feeling he's a pompous, probably elderly Scot with a penchant for tartan—and a penchant for doing things on the cheap—so the answer's no.'

'In other words,' Delia said calmly, 'you'd like me to write a polite note to the effect that prior commitments force you to decline his most flattering commission with deep regret.'

Saffron's lips quivered. 'Precisely. I don't know what I'd do without you, Delia!'

Delia shrugged. 'It's almost true. We're virtually snowed under, but—sure you don't want to think it over at least?'

Saffron regarded her assistant with affection. Delia was forty-five to Saffron's twenty-five, childless, with a failed marriage behind her, and she threw all the energy she might have given to a family into her work. Delia is not artistic but a genius at law and order, as Saffron thought of it: keeping the books, chasing up recalcitrant suppliers, defining priorities and so on.

Delia is also, Saffron mused, a genius at calming my own more flamboyant, not to say totally mad moments, and I don't know what I'd do without her. All the same…

'No, Delia. I just don't think I can find the time to do a job that far away, considering the logistics of it, which are bound to be complicated. And, to be honest, I do have the feeling this job is not for me, don't ask me why.'

She grimaced and picked up the letter again then flipped it with the back of her hand. 'He's got to be old—the language is so archaic and...and patronising!'

Delia rescued the letter and read it again. '"Please be so good as to let us have your immediate response"...I guess so. All the same—'

'I know,' Saffron interrupted. 'We both know some wonderful old people, but no. Fraser *A*. Ross and I are not for one another; trust me.'

'All right. Uh—you haven't forgotten you're invited to Judge and Mrs Whitney Spence's dinner dance on Friday night, have you? It's almost in honour of you since you redecorated their house.'

'Yes, I had—damn,' Saffron said gloomily. 'I haven't a thing to wear!'

'Then go out and get yourself something,' Delia recommended unsympathetically. 'I'm sure it will be very haute couture.'

Saffron brightened. 'Make a statement, you mean?'

'Why not?' Delia replied. 'We *both* know how much you enjoy that.' Her eyes softened as her boss looked hurt. She added, 'You can also afford to now, through your own hard work, your talent, and, I have to say, a very good business head on your shoulders.'

'I am unmanned!' Saffron murmured, and they both dissolved into laughter again.

But after Delia had left her Saffron sat for a few

moments with her chin in her hands and thought back over the last few years.

She recalled how she'd started her business doing, of all things, marine upholstery. She'd not then had this shop at Sanctuary Cove—a lovely resort, shopping village and residential estate at the northern end of the Gold Coast. She had in fact operated out of a one-bedroomed flat in Southport with one eccentric industrial sewing machine, although she'd had, by way of training, two years at a college where she'd studied art, design, textile manufacture and interior decorating.

She'd always loved to draw and had always been fascinated by colour co-ordination, houses, furniture, antiques and modern art.

And because Sanctuary Cove was situated on the Coomera river and had a large marina this was where she'd come to look for business, and to coin a phrase, she thought with a faint smile, one thing had led to another.

A few discreet suggestions to some of the yacht owners she'd worked for had resulted in her being commissioned not only to re-cover their upholstery but also to redecorate their entire interiors. And word had spread. Sanctuary Cove had been growing at an astonishing rate—house and condominium-wise—and before very long she had got her first commission to do an entire house.

About two years later, she'd had enough work to give away the fiddly, difficult work of marine upholstery and to open The Crocus Shop right here in the village. Nor was she confined to Sanctuary Cove now;

her talents were sought all over the Gold Coast and hinterland, and up to Brisbane.

But she never regretted being based in the village. She loved its atmosphere, the shops, the art gallery, the restaurants and pavement cafés. Then there was the market and the movie theatre, the lovely view over the river of all the yachts and sleek motor cruisers, the eclectic mixture of yachties, tourists and all the people who lived at Sanctuary Cove.

The gardens were always lush and beautiful. There were two golf courses, facilities such as the Recreation Club—which she belonged to—where you could play not only golf but tennis, work out in the gym if you were so inclined, or cool off in the swimming pool after a long, hot day. And there were often village events such as bands and concerts over the weekends, fashion parades, the boat show, the Christmas carols and so on.

No, Saffron thought, Sanctuary Cove has been very, very good to me, and she pulled her sketch pad back in front of her.

But it wasn't until Friday lunchtime, four days later, that Saffron remembered her decision to make a fashion statement that night, and she rushed out to do some shopping. The dress she took home with her was a dream. She also finished work early for once and took some time to pamper herself for the party. She took a long, dreamy bubble bath then washed her hair.

While it dried, she relaxed in a comfortable chair and did her nails, painting their short, perfectly filed ovals in a fashionable French nude pink. When they were dry, she started to dress, putting on a frivolous lacy suspender belt and drawing on the sheerest of stockings. Matching silk and lace briefs completed her underwear, for her dress had a built-in bra. Then she reached for the dress and breathed with satisfaction because it was such a thing of beauty...

'Who's the pocket Venus?'

Diana Marr looked up and followed her brother's idle, oddly dispassionate gaze. 'Ah, that's...' But she paused suddenly then said stringently, 'Not for you.'

'No?' He raised a wry eyebrow. 'Why on earth not?'

Diana chewed her lip and watched Saffron, who glowed in the palest sea-green silk organza ballgown. It was strapless, clung to her bust and highlighted her tiny waist before falling in stiff, rich folds to just above the floor. With it she wore a delicate seven-strand bead necklace that fell to her waist, the beads matching both her dress and her eyes. Her long, curly russet hair was loose and natural. When she moved, it could be seen that she was wearing very high-heeled backless shoes with ballerina ribbons criss-crossed about her slender ankles.

And Diana Marr, dressed more conservatively, and much more appropriately for what was a dinner dance and *not* a grand ball, had to concede with a sigh that Saffron Shaw had stolen the show.

'Diana?' her brother prompted mildly.

'She's just not your type.'

'You're an authority on that, dear sister mine?'

'Yes,' Diana said crossly. 'She's a very cool, shrewd businesswoman; she's dedicated to her career,

I'm sure. And you should be looking for a *wife*, not a—'

'The other kind of woman?' her brother interposed with a grin. 'But I am.'

Diana's eyes flew to his and disturbed only a deeply grave look in their dark depths. Which, having known him all her life, she mistrusted devoutly. 'No, look, I'm serious,' she said hotly. 'You're thirty-five—'

'One-foot-in-the-grave material at least,' he murmured.

'You know what I mean!' Diana clicked her tongue exasperatedly. 'You—'

'I know exactly what you mean, beloved,' her infuriating brother soothed. 'But, believe me, I'm serious too. A wife is very definitely what I need and indeed am looking for.'

Diana opened her mouth, closed it, then said tartly, 'Why don't you advertise?'

He grinned down at her. 'Now *why* did I think you'd approve?'

'I do. I'm just not sure that's how it works. But if you *are* serious, I'd stay away from Saffron Shaw.'

'Ah. So that's Saffron Shaw.'

Something in his tone made Diana study her brother again with a slight frown. And it irked her severely as she did so to know that his dark, satanic good looks were diabolically irresistible to women; she'd seen it so many times before. Not only that, she'd gone out of her way to draw to his attention several candidates who would have made fine wives for him, but nothing had ever come of it!

'That's Saffron,' she agreed shortly. 'She's just re-decorated this house.'

'Very impressive.' He glanced around.

'Yes. The Spences are besotted.'

'But obviously not you, Diana,' he drawled. 'Why don't you spell out in words of one syllable why she should be stayed away from? Before you burst a gasket,' he added softly.

'There are times when I hate you,' Diana stated.

'Come on, Di,' he cajoled with a sudden charming smile. 'Is she, let's say, promiscuous? Already married? Divorced? What else could she have done to earn your disapproval?'

Diana coloured faintly. 'Nothing that I know of,' she said stiffly, then relented a little to add candidly, 'And I probably *would* know. No, she's just extremely wrapped up in her work!'

'She looks anything but at the moment,' her brother commented rather dryly as Saffron danced past in the arms of a man she was talking to vivaciously at the same time as they whirled and twirled to the music.

'But that's just it, don't you see?' Diana said heatedly. 'It's *advertising*. She's managed to eclipse the lot of us and no one will leave here tonight without knowing who she is.'

'So, yes, I do see,' her brother said after a moment, directing a wickedly knowing little look down at his sister in her matronly although very expensive beige dress.

Diana Marr closed her eyes and said through her teeth, 'I'm not jealous— Oh, all right! We probably all are! Satisfied?'

*   *   *

The first intimation that Diana Marr's brother had any interest in her came to Saffron in the form of having him tap her dancing partner on the shoulder, who then surrendered her to this tall, dark stranger.

Not willingly, mind you, and, in the rueful process of changing over, he did say, 'Now you watch yourself, Saffron!' before he regretfully left her to her fate.

Damn, Saffron thought as she was gathered into a pair of strong arms, I was enjoying myself! She looked coolly up into a pair of lazy dark eyes and said equally coolly, 'Who are you?'

'A perfect stranger?' her new partner suggested, and for some reason there was a hint of irony in those eyes.

Saffron narrowed her own eyes and considered. There was no doubt he was tall, dark and good-looking, and that his beautifully tailored charcoal suit with a discreet pinstripe highlighted rather than hid broad shoulders and a lean, strong, honed body. There was no doubt that he was on the receiving end of some admiring glances from women dancing past. No doubt that he was very much at ease in this milieu— a legal eagle? she wondered briefly. And no doubting at all that he was amused by her coolness.

'Perfect?' she murmured. 'That's open to two interpretations, isn't it?'

'A *complete* stranger, then,' he agreed. 'Is that a problem?'

'Yes, it is,' she answered swiftly. 'I don't enjoy dancing with complete strangers.'

He raised a dark eyebrow at her and swung her round in perfect time to the music. 'Something wrong with my dancing?'

Saffron gritted her teeth. There was nothing wrong with his dancing at all. Few men she'd danced with had danced better, in fact, or handled her as lightly and expertly for that matter. 'No,' she said baldly.

'Then it must be me,' he murmured, and laughed down at her in a way that curiously affected her heartbeat.

What is this? she found herself wondering. How can a man in a matter of moments make you feel like this? Because, she answered herself, you're not a naive little girl, Saffron. And there's something in the way those dark eyes linger on you that's rather explicit. Which caused her to say tartly, 'It must be.'

'Because we haven't been introduced?' he surmised. 'I can remedy that now—'

'It doesn't matter.'

'I see,' he murmured, not in the least perturbed, apparently. 'Very well; I'll consider myself rapped on the knuckles. By the way, your dress was an inspired choice.' He glanced downwards.

Quite sure that he was going to comment on the strapless nature of her dress, Saffron clenched her teeth. But as their gazes clashed again he said simply, 'It matches your eyes.'

Surprise held her silent, and he went on, 'Tell me about yourself. I believe you're responsible for all this—magnificence.' He looked around wryly.

'Magnificence?' she responded immediately and with a haughty toss of her head. 'You say that as if I've gone overboard.'

'Oh, not for the Spences, I'm sure.'

'Well, you're right,' she conceded after a taut pause during which honesty prevailed, and she couldn't resist a deep little chuckle. 'To tell you the truth, it's only due to my restraining influence that this is not a miniversion of the Palace of Versailles. Are you not a friend of the Spences?' she added, suddenly regretting any semblance of easy intimacy with this man.

'I most certainly am. That doesn't blind me to their delusions of grandeur, however. It must have been quite a coup, getting this job.'

'And it's just occurred to me that you know who I am,' Saffron countered.

'Doesn't everyone? I'm assured that they do. Most of the women are green with envy, incidentally. Do you think that's entirely wise?'

Saffron stopped dancing. 'Wise?'

'From a business point of view. Jealous wives can be a problem, can't they?' he said mildly.

Saffron's mouth fell open and he took the opportunity to lead her smoothly into the dance again. He also said, 'Just thought I'd point it out. I believe your business is your life, sort of thing.' He glanced down at her enquiringly. 'Although I must say it seems an awful waste.'

Her teeth clicked audibly as she shut her mouth. 'Well, you've got one thing right—my business is my life. And if you're offering to help me change that, Mr Complete Stranger, thanks, but no, thanks!'

But again he laughed down at her, and again her heartbeat altered and she tripped suddenly, causing him to gather her closer and slow the pace at the same time.

'All right?' he said, barely audibly.

Saffron stared up into his dark eyes and, although she'd often regretted being only five feet two, it sud-

denly and crazily didn't matter a bit, it was even nice
to be in the arms of a tall man. It made her feel delicate.

And, she thought with a pang, it's not only his
smile that makes my heart go bang—it's his height
and those broad shoulders and the clever lines of his
face... It's the clean, starchy smell of a crackling-
crisp cotton shirt beneath his jacket, and beneath that
just the scent of pure man, with no aftershave, only
soap...

What would he be like to go to bed with? she wondered. What would you feel if he slid your dress
down, uncovering your breasts, and all you had on
was—virtually nothing? Vulnerable? Afraid? Or
proud and curious and deliciously sensuous?

'Saffron?'

She started but couldn't tear her eyes from his, nor
rid herself of the image of the two of them in some
quiet, very private place undressing each other
slowly. Indeed as they stared at each other they might
have been a million miles from Judge and Mrs
Whitney Spence's dinner dance. And the silk organza
of her beautiful gown might have been gossamer
gauze where his hands rested on it, and her body beneath it thrilled to the touch.

'I thought so,' he said, almost gently.

'Thought what?' Her voice sounded tiny and far
away.

'That there's more to you than business, Saffron.
And if I can't have one why not the other?'

'I don't know what you mean...' But all of a sudden sanity returned. Sanity that told her this *was* a
complete stranger and, not only that, one who had

laughed at her, insulted her... 'How *dare* you?' she whispered, and twitched herself out of his arms.

It helped not one whit to hear his low laughter as she stalked away.

The evening was spoilt, however, she discovered, although she mixed, was complimented and even fêted for her redecoration of the Spence house.

It was spoilt for several reasons—who *was* he, for one? But nothing gave her a clue and she was determined not to ask. Had he been serious about jealous wives? And, if so, what had prompted it? *Had* she gone overboard with her dress—was that it? She even found herself looking around at her own interior decorating once, and loathing it.

All of which contrived to bother and upset her so much that she refused every other offer to dance and found herself steering clear of husbands even only in conversation. Whereas her complete stranger, from what she saw of him, didn't give her another thought or glance.

Which was why Diana Marr came to find her sitting alone on a gold brocade settee, deep in thought. 'Saffron? Not dancing any more?'

'Oh—hello, Diana. No.'

'Mind if I join you, then?'

'Not at all.' Saffron moved up politely. She didn't know Diana that well, other than that she moved in the very best circles and was reputed to belong to a very wealthy family. Her husband was a stockbroker.

'You must be very proud,' Diana said now, bestowing a friendly smile upon Saffron.

'Oh?'

'To be so young and so successful,' Diana elaborated, and waved a hand. 'Whitney and Sarah are absolutely delighted with their house.'

'Thank you,' Saffron said, and grimaced at the gloomy note she caught in her voice.

'Such a pity you couldn't take on my brother's decorating but I'm sure he understands—particularly after seeing how sought after you are now. I've heard at least six people beg you to do their houses tonight alone!'

Saffron frowned. 'Your brother?'

'Yes—and, talk of the devil, here he is!'

Saffron looked up and went cold. 'He's your brother?'

'For my sins, yes,' Diana said gaily. 'Didn't he introduce himself? I saw you dancing.'

'I wasn't allowed to,' the man who was no longer a complete stranger said, and sat down opposite in an armchair. 'Was I, Saffron?'

She swallowed and fiddled with her beads. 'I...uh... Well, so you're a Marr,' she said feebly and idiotically. 'But I don't remember—'

'Oh, he's not a Marr, darling.' Diana chuckled although she looked faintly surprised. 'Pure Ross, Fraser is.'

For the second time that night Saffron's mouth fell open, which Fraser Ross watched with a little gleam of pure amusement in his dark eyes. Then she said hoarsely, 'Fraser A. Ross?'

He nodded politely.

'But that's ridiculous; you can't be!' The words burst out before Saffron could help herself, and she was often to wonder if she would forget until her dying day saying something so stupid.

'In what respect can't I be?' Fraser Ross enquired gravely.

'Well...well...' she floundered '...I thought you must be older.'

'Ah. Now why would you think that, I wonder?'

Saffron breathed deeply. 'The tone of your letter, your initial.' Which sounded even worse, but again she couldn't retract the words.

'Is that why you knocked me back?' He grinned satanically. 'Well, I can put that right—as you see I haven't got one foot in the grave.' For some reason he looked at his sister ironically. 'And I use the A because my father is also Fraser Ross. As for the tone of my letter, we have a very faithful family retainer who does my private secretarial work when I'm here. She's at least seventy, but none of us have the heart to turn her off.'

'Of course, all of that is academic,' Diana Marr put in a little hastily. 'Saffron is just too busy, aren't you, dear?'

'Of course,' Fraser Ross murmured. 'Unless you'd care to reconsider, Saffron? For purely business reasons naturally.'

But there was nothing businesslike in his swift dark glance that took in the smooth, bare skin of her neck and shoulders, her cleavage and slender waist, and even her slender ankles exposed in their criss-crossed ribbons by the way she sat.

Oh, no, she thought. That searing little glance is designed to do one thing—remind me of how it felt to stand in the circle of his arms, literally breathing and drinking him in.

She stood up, and with almost regal care settled her

beads and smoothed the flow of her skirt. Then she clasped her hands loosely in front of her and said quite audibly, and with not the slightest tinge of regret, '*I* choose my clients, Mr Ross, not the other way around. And I never choose clients who attempt to proposition me or badger me or generally make a nuisance of themselves. So once again thanks, but *no*, thanks!'

She walked away with her head held high, her back straight and her eyes flashing green sparks.

'I can't believe I did it—not that I regret it!' Saffron said to Delia the next morning.

'Perish the thought,' Delia murmured.

'It's just, well, when I walked away—that was when I realised how many people were in earshot, you see. I mean, they parted for me like the Red Sea! And they were all—agog.'

'Embarrassing?' Delia suggested cautiously.

Saffron looked haughty. 'Not at the time, no. In fact I was so annoyed I just kept on walking.' She shrugged. 'Right out of the party.'

'So you didn't say goodbye or thank you or anything?'

'No. Although I have sent flowers and an apology this morning.'

'That'll probably take care of the Spences' wounded feelings.'

'I hope so. Do you know, he even had the gall to intimate that I'd gone over the top with their house?'

'You were a bit worried about that yourself,' Delia pointed out. 'Then you decided if that's what they wanted that's what they should have.'

'I know. I wish I hadn't.' Saffron sighed deeply and looked around as if to reassure herself.

The Crocus Shop consisted of a small showroom facing the pavement with two offices behind. The showroom this month—she changed the display every month—featured the mock corner of a morning room with a deliciously and plumply padded armchair that made you long to sink into it just looking at it. It was covered in wisteria-blue linen patterned with cream and yellow irises.

And beside it was an antique desk with elegantly curved legs and lots of little drawers. A most fitting desk for the lady of the manor to conduct her house-hold business from. A stubby crystal vase of fresh irises in cream, yellow and violet was kept on the desk.

Saffron could not actually see this display from her office but it comforted her to know it was there.

Her office also reassured her. The walls were papered in thick, matt corn-gold, and her huge desk was also an antique. Lovely green-framed prints and paintings hung on three walls and on the fourth was a magnificent woven wall-hanging of crocuses on a soft green background that matched the carpet. She sat in a buttoned, forest-green velvet chair with wooden legs, as did Delia across the desk from her.

'I've found out a bit more about him,' Delia said then, with a keen little look at her boss.

'I don't want to hear it.'

'All right. Look, this fabric for the Johnson house is no longer available so—'

'Yes, I do,' Saffron said fatalistically. 'Then I can hate him wholeheartedly.'

Delia laughed. 'They have a finger in most pies, the Ross family. A chain of retail stores, a freight haulage company, a fleet of prawn trawlers, a charter boat company, hotels—'

'OK, I get the picture,' Saffron said gloomily.

'Well, Fraser B. Ross suffered some serious ill health a few years back and handed over the reins to his son—'

'Fraser A.'

'The same. Incidentally, the B stands for Bernard and the A stands for Andrew.'

'How original,' Saffron said scathingly. 'Would it be too much to hope that he's squandered the family fortune, that he's the black sheep of the family and a notorious rake?'

'Yes,' Delia said simply, then amended it. 'Well, I don't know about the rake bit. He's not married, although he's thirty-five, but if anything he's extended the family fortune since he took over.'

'How come we'd never heard of him?'

Delia frowned. 'He guards his privacy very strictly. His sister, by the way, is his only sibling, and there are rumours that her marriage is not very happy.'

Saffron considered. 'I think she was on her own last night, now you come to mention it. And, now I come to think of it, I've met Roger Marr, and got the impression he has a roving eye. I wonder if *she* typified the jealous wife Mr Fraser A. Ross just thought to mention? How *do* you know all this, by the way, Delia? If he guards his privacy so well?'

'I just happen to have a friend who works for the morning paper. They generally know everyone who is anyone, and all the gossip too.'

'I wish you'd told me this *before* last night.'

'Didn't know you were liable to bump into him, did I?' Delia said calmly.

'All the same, what made you want to know more about the man?'

'I don't know.' Delia paused and frowned. 'For some reason I had a feeling about that job. But you have to admit you did too, even if for all the wrong reasons.'

Saffron ground her teeth audibly. Then she grinned suddenly. 'Pompous, parsimonious, elderly, with a penchant for tartan—how wrong could you be? Oh, well, you win some and you lose some. But there are some very *right* reasons why I could never work with Fraser A. Ross so I don't think I'll lose any more sleep over it!'

'Not even if I tell you I don't like tartan?' a strange voice, but one that Saffron remembered all too well, asked amusedly.

CHAPTER TWO

IT AMUSED him, as he stood at the doorway of what was the inner sanctum of The Crocus Shop, to see Saffron Shaw lift her head incredulously and regard him once again with her mouth open.

'How do you do?' He extended his hand to Delia. 'I'm Fraser Ross. I apologise for the misleading impression my letter gave you both. That I must be pompous, parsimonious—not to mention elderly—and with a penchant for tartan,' he added gently.

'You—you've been eavesdropping!' Saffron got out as Delia shook the hand held out to her with a tinge of colour entering her cheeks.

'I just thought I'd make my presence known. I have been waiting outside for a couple of minutes.'

'It's Saturday. We are closed to the public,' Saffron said arctically.

'Then mightn't it be a good idea to put up a "closed" sign and lock the door?' he suggested.

'I did lock the door,' Delia said, 'but—' She paused and glanced at Saffron.

'All *right*. I came in after you and forgot to lock it again, I suppose,' Saffron said crossly. 'That doesn't mean to say—'

'Why don't I make us some coffee?' Delia put in smoothly. She got up and, with a courtly gesture, offered Fraser Ross her chair across the desk from

Saffron. 'Won't take a minute,' she added, and glided out.

'How very kind of her,' he murmured, sitting down easily and disposing of a slim briefcase. Then, with that lazy glance she was coming to know, he looked across the desk.

She looked younger this morning, he thought at the same time. Those luxurious curls were severely pulled back in upward wings and the rest of her rich russet locks were neatly plaited and bound at the bottom with a narrow ribbon. There were slight blue shadows beneath her eyes, but the autocratic little nose had lost none of its hauteur.

She was simply dressed in a voluminous green cotton overshirt and, from what he could see beneath the desk, green leggings splashed with white daisies, and green sand-shoes splashed with paint.

As Saffron realised the kind of scrutiny she was being subjected to, she heard herself say tartly and foolishly again, 'It *is* Saturday…' then bit her lip vexedly.

'Of course,' he agreed. 'I haven't bothered to dress up either. Is that what you mean?'

She looked at him dryly. His form of not dressing up was a bit different from her leggings and favourite old sand-shoes. His form of not dressing up consisted of navy trousers and a pumpkin-yellow T-shirt with a navy collar, all of it impeccably laundered and pressed, all of it shouting the finest quality. And all of it once again emphasising the lean, long, broad-shouldered elegance of his body. His thick dark hair was brushed and tidy and he looked freshly shaved.

He also, she suddenly thought, had the kind of

Celtic darkness that went well with his name: a slightly olive skin, an aura of—what? she wondered. The aura of a man not to be trifled with but a man who could set your soul singing? Because of those dark and often amused eyes, those beautiful hands.

She suddenly realised he was looking at her with a wryly raised eyebrow. 'What I really mean, Mr Ross,' she said coldly, 'is this: why are you here? I thought I made it perfectly plain—'

'Do you mean perfectly or completely?'

'Don't quibble,' she warned through her teeth.

'But aren't you into semantics?' he drawled. 'Perfect strangers or complete strangers—that kind of thing?'

'Then I'll rephrase. I am not going to decorate your holiday home!'

'Because I propositioned you?' He smiled slightly. 'After all, there's nothing left to accuse me of now, not of your original quibbles anyway.' He raised a mocking eyebrow at her. 'Oh, by the way, I'm not mean, Saffron, in any respect.'

'It's much simpler,' she said after a taut moment during which she reined in her temper with a visible effort. 'I'm very busy; I'm so busy I don't know which way to turn. As Delia—' she looked up gratefully as Delia came in with the coffee '—will be able to confirm. *Won't* you, Delia?' she said sternly, with a warning glint in her green eyes.

'We certainly do have a lot on our plate at the moment,' Delia agreed as she distributed a cafetière of aromatic coffee and two attractive green pottery mugs splashed with crocus flowers. She also put down cream, milk and sugar and a plate of iced bakery biscuits. She then straightened and added, 'However, with a bit of judicious rearranging, we might just be able to fit it in. Enjoy the coffee.'

'Perhaps I should pour,' Fraser Ross said a few moments later when Saffron was still regarding the empty doorway with disbelief. 'We wouldn't want it to go cold. Seeing as she went to so much trouble.'

Saffron withdrew her gaze from the door but was further incensed on seeing his barely hidden laughter. 'Look here, *I* make the decisions!'

'Well, it's funny you should say that,' he murmured, politely handing her the milk and sugar. 'I was led to believe you were a dedicated businesswoman— a very shrewd one too.'

'You wouldn't be sitting here otherwise,' Saffron observed acidly. 'Which is exactly why I can pick and choose who I—'

'Ah.' He sat back and stirred his coffee thoughtfully. 'I think that's something we ought to discuss.'

'What do you mean? I don't understand.'

'Just this. Not doing my house could affect your future business—prospects.'

For some reason, Saffron put her hands around her mug to warm them although it was not a cold day. But there was a distinctly cold feeling running down her spine as well and it came from the way Fraser Ross was now looking at her. Still amusedly, yes, but there was something else in those dark eyes, something faintly ironic, something that made her think of a cat-and-mouse situation—with herself featuring as the mouse.

Don't be ridiculous, Saffron, she advised herself,

and sat up proudly. 'Oh? And just how could that happen, Mr Ross?'

He waved a lean, strong hand with its sprinkle of black hairs on the back. 'A few words in a few ears, Saffron. That's all it would take.'

She gasped. 'Do you mean to say—? You *wouldn't*! You couldn't!'

'Influence people against you? I'm afraid I could,' he said regretfully. 'And I'm afraid my sister could do so even more successfully. She doesn't altogether like you, you see. She certainly doesn't like being eclipsed the way she was last night.'

'I…' Saffron stared at him wide-eyed.

'Unfortunately my sister is in a slightly ambivalent mood these days,' he continued wryly. 'As you so rightly heard and perceived, her marriage is unhappy and her husband undoubtedly has a roving eye—'

'I…you…I have *never*… What is this?' Saffron finished disjointedly.

'I'm sure you haven't, otherwise your business would have already fallen off dramatically,' he said ruefully. 'But unfortunately choosing to assume a high profile, whilst certainly having its advertising potential, can also lay you open to all sorts of speculation.'

'I don't believe this,' Saffron said flatly.

'If I were you, I would.'

'Then I'll tell you what I do believe,' she said slowly and carefully. 'That you have a very large and fragile ego, Mr Ross. Did I dent it when I accused you, rightfully, of trying to proposition me last night? Dear me, how sad,' she said gently.

'What is actually sadder, Saffron,' he remarked

equally and lethally as gently, 'is that you melted in my arms last night as we *both* discovered a wakening and spontaneous interest in each other—then you chose to deny it. Did you dent my ego? Sure.' He grinned reminiscently. 'But I'm told I'm not one to let a, let's say, a provocation like that go by unchallenged.'

'It wasn't a provocation! I meant it!'

'Whatever,' he murmured.

'The...the Spences,' she spluttered. 'They would always stand up for me!'

'Whitney and Sarah?' he mused. 'Do you know, they were just a little put out that such an old friend of the family should have been publicly insulted by someone who, after all, is only the interior decorator?'

Saffron sat back and slammed her mug onto the desk so that coffee spilt over the top. 'Now listen to me,' she said fiercely, then changed tack at a sudden thought. 'Talk about insults! *You* were the one who mentioned their delusions of grandeur!'

'When you're in the inner circle, you can get away with things like that,' he said lightly.

Saffron slammed her chair back this time and got up to prowl the office like a caged tiger. 'The answer is still no,' she tossed over her shoulder. 'People can either take me or leave me. My future will rest on my ability.'

'Things don't always work that way. Do you know what you remind me of? An enraged kitten,' he said softly. 'Look,' he added comfortably, 'not only could you mend the fences you slightly smashed last night if you did my house, but you could enhance your reputation considerably.'

'A holiday home stuck away on an island?' she said derisively and unwisely.

'One that a lot of people will get to see,' he replied. 'One that some of the finest materials have been used to build, designed by one of our most exciting architects, and one that some of the finest interior decorating magazines are panting to get on their pages.'

She paused and swung to face him. 'You wouldn't want to be splashed on the pages of a magazine—not Fraser A. Ross who apparently goes out of his way to guard his privacy!' she said scornfully.

'If you could see your way to decorating it, I could see my way to it being in at least one such publication.'

Saffron leant against the wall and stared at Fraser Ross narrowly. Why was he doing this? she wondered. Had she jolted his ego that badly? It didn't make sense. The man was a millionaire, and good-looking enough anyway not to have to resort to blackmail because she'd dented his ego. There must be women flocking after him, she mused. But could he and would he carry out his threat if she refused?

Something in the way he accepted her scrutiny with polite yet supreme indifference told her he could. Yet it wasn't the thought of all the hardship she'd endured to get this far that prompted her decision—it was quite simply a sudden and overwhelming desire to meet and beat this man at his own game.

She straightened abruptly and strode over to her chair. 'OK. On one condition.'

It was his turn to study her narrowly, and comment dryly, 'I wonder what brought that little gleam to your eyes, Saffron?'

She grimaced and shrugged. 'Dollar signs twirling around like a fruit machine?' she suggested.

He was silent for a moment, then he went on, 'I think I can guess your condition—no more propositioning, that kind of thing?' His dark eyes mocked her.

'Not at all—that is to say, you guessed wrong,' she replied. '"That kind of thing" won't be a problem because you just won't have the opportunity. No, I'll take the job provided I can do it now, and do it fast.'

'A rushed, botched decorating job was not what I had in mind,' he murmured.

'Beggars—surely a misleading term in this instance—can't be choosers, Mr Ross,' she said briskly. 'I start a major project in three weeks. In the interim, with Delia's judicious rearranging—' she looked irritably at the door '—I can fit you in before it. There's no chance after that for at least three months—I *am* exceedingly busy.'

'I see.'

She clicked her teeth exasperatedly. 'Don't say that as if you don't believe a word I'm saying. I tell you I have a posh new guest house coming up with twenty-five bedrooms that all have to be different!'

'I'm impressed.'

'I should hope so.' She subsided somewhat then added, 'But you shouldn't worry; *I'm* at my best when presented with a challenge.' A little glint of pure malice lit her green eyes. 'And to do a job in three weeks would certainly be one. Let's say the ideas seem to flow under pressure.'

'Is that so?'

'Yes. Take it or leave it,' she said simply, and pulled a calculator towards her. 'I'm also expensive.'

'I didn't doubt that.'

She glanced upwards swiftly because the tone of his voice suggested a *double entendre*, but he met her gaze innocently. All the same, her nostrils pinched slightly and her mouth set in a line.

But before she could speak he said, 'I'm only surprised you haven't got around to asking for carte blanche.'

'What kind of a fool do you take me for, Mr Ross?' She tilted her chin at him imperiously.

He smiled slightly. 'I don't know; you tell me.'

'Would you be prepared to sign a contract to that effect?'

'No.'

'Then I have no intention of fighting you through the courts for years because you could claim I haven't interpreted your wishes. No. I work differently. At each stage you give me your approval or otherwise.'

'Very wise,' he agreed. 'It'll also give us the opportunity to get to know each other better, won't it?' He raised a wry eyebrow at her.

'That wasn't my intention,' she stated icily.

'Perhaps not,' he agreed again.

'You really are—' Saffron broke off as he stood up.

'Yes, Miss Shaw?'

'*Annoying,*' she said. 'And if you think towering over me is going to intimidate me in the slightest, you had best—'

'As a matter of fact, intimidation wasn't what I had in mind, Saffron,' he drawled. 'I was merely wondering what you would do if I kissed you. Continue to spit at me like an outraged kitten? Or melt in my arms again and contemplate other...intimate little pleasures we could indulge in?'

The colour that poured into her cheeks told its own tale. 'I didn't—'

'Oh, yes, you did,' he contradicted her softly, and touched a careless finger to her hot cheek. Then he bent down to retrieve his briefcase which he opened and withdrew a packet from.

'L-look,' she stammered, and stopped.

'Going to chicken out?' he suggested lazily.

Saffron breathed deeply. '*No.*'

'Good.' He tapped the packet. 'These are the plans and some photos. Spend the afternoon with them then come and have dinner with me. We can work out a plan of action.'

'I would sooner have dinner with a—snake,' she said.

'Would you?' He grinned. 'Sorry but I don't think I can arrange it. If you're expressing a concern for your safety, though, my father will be present, and interested to meet you. The address is on the packet. Say seven-thirty? See you this evening, Saffron.' He strolled to the door then turned back to her. 'By the way, this will be an *informal* dinner. You won't need to dress up—or should I say down?' He left with a mocking little smile.

Delia was unfortunate enough to come in a moment later.

'This is all your fault!' Saffron said stormily.

'You've agreed to do it? Very wise,' Delia replied placidly.

Saffron swore beneath her breath. 'It's not wise at all; the man is—'

'The man is something else?' Delia suggested with a little twinkle.

'Impossible.' Saffron ripped open the packet, more as a way to relieve her feelings than because she was interested in the contents, and a river of glossy photos fell out.

'He's...he's,' she continued, not deigning to look at the photos, 'actually blackmailed me into doing it, Delia! He threatened to...to blacken my name amongst all his wealthy friends. He's got the Spences feeling that I behaved badly last night—*I* behaved badly! And his sister, who *is* going through the mill with her husband, will be happy to help him.'

Delia grimaced. 'Sounds as if he's carrying a few loaded pistols. What exactly *did* you do last night?'

Saffron opened her mouth then closed it. In her description of the events to Delia, she'd glossed over the precise nature of what had occurred between herself and Fraser A. Ross beyond stating merely that he'd propositioned her. 'Why do you automatically imagine *I* did something?' she asked abruptly and indignantly.

'Because I know you well enough to know that you don't, as a rule, take things lying down, Saffron,' Delia said honestly. 'And it seems a bit extreme for a man to go to these lengths, especially a man with all the resources of Fraser Ross.' She waited with a lifted eyebrow.

'I...' Saffron shrugged '...dented his ego.'

'Quite badly?'

'So it would seem.'

'So it would.' Delia hid a smile. 'Never mind; just think of the kudos that might come your way with this job.'

'That's exactly what he said.' Saffron stared affrontedly at the crocuses on the wall. Then she looked at Delia with more spirit. 'You do realise how much work I've let us in for? I said I would have to do it in the next three weeks.'

'Good thinking,' Delia murmured. 'Once you start on the new guest house—'

'Well, I'll tell you what, Delia,' Saffron interrupted. 'You can come to dinner with him tonight, too. I'll need your level head and all the rest of it.'

'But—have I been invited? Have *you* been invited?' For a moment Delia looked thrown off course.

'Of course I've been invited! You don't think I'd invite myself to dinner with the b—man? As a matter of fact I wasn't invited,' she amended, causing Delia to look more confused. 'I was commanded. But I shouldn't imagine Fraser *A*. Ross couldn't scrape up an extra plate.'

'But...but where?'

'Haven't the faintest; he said the address was on the packet.' She turned the packet over and looked up triumphantly. 'Would you believe it, Delia, dear? He lives right here at Sanctuary Cove!'

'All the same, I don't... Saffron?'

But Saffron didn't answer as she finally took note of the photos and started to flip through them.

'Saffron?' Delia said again after a few minutes, during which she watched her boss's eye take on an entirely different expression.

'*Java*,' Saffron replied, and added earnestly,

'Didn't that shop at Marina Mirage just get in a new consignment of Javanese furniture? It'd be *perfect*. Look at this, Delia,' she said excitedly.

But Delia looked at Saffron instead. Affectionately and with some relief. 'Whatever you say, Saffron. Shall I pick you up tonight?'

It was six-thirty when Saffron got home.

She not only worked at Sanctuary Cove but lived there in a two-bedroomed, two-storeyed golf-course condominium. Not that she played golf but it was ideally situated in that she could walk to work, and the views overlooking the sweeping green fairways were lovely. Normally, coming home to it was a pleasure.

She'd decorated most of it simply and with a Mediterranean flavour. Polished stone floors with rugs rather than fitted carpet. Mushroom-coloured walls and dusky blue panelled doors, louvred shutters or natural canvas blinds. There was unfussy furniture with the emphasis on lovely woods, and a divinely comfortable couch in the lounge with lots of cushions and covered in a rich buttermilk cotton damask.

Her bedroom was different. It was all off-white—walls, curtains and carpet—but the double bed was covered in a spread that was a riot of spring flowers—violets, crocuses, jonquils, lilies of the valley. There was a lovely old rocker and a delicate, dark wood antique dressing table with a square mirror and, on its polished surface, silver framed photos and a bowl of fragrant pot-pourri.

But Saffron didn't pause to enjoy the soothing visual aspects of her bedroom; she walked straight through to her walk-in wardrobe that led to the *en suite* bathroom, muttering to herself along the lines of, '*In*formal! OK, Mr Fraser Ross!'

She scanned the hanging clothes, but the first thing her eyes fell on was the gown she'd worn last night to the Spences' dinner dance and she regarded it warily for a moment. Had it been a mistake? *Something* she'd done had to have been a mistake to cause her this kind of contretemps. But just the sight of the dress, she found, was enough to call to mind being in his arms...

She wandered away from the wardrobe and stood before her bedroom window with her arms folded and a frown in her eyes. Had it been the mutual discovery of a wakening and spontaneous interest in each other? Well, he did manage to awaken something in you, Saffron, you have to admit, she told herself. Something you'd hoped was, if not dead, certainly dormant. Since Simon.

She turned away with a sigh then thought, Anyway, you're entitled to be extremely wary of a strange man doing anything to you. What does it point to? A very practised operator, probably, that's all I mean, why would I believe Fraser *A.* Ross took one look at me and was smitten?

You're right, she told herself, and advanced to the walk-in wardrobe again.

Ten minutes later she was attired informally and Delia arrived, who said cautiously, 'Saffron—are you *mad*?'

'No. Why?'

'What are you wearing, then?'

'What does it look like?'

'A boiler suit?'

Saffron giggled. 'It's a flying suit actually. Very roomy and comfortable.' She twirled around in the baggy khaki one-piece outfit with its multitude of pockets, its long sleeves and legs, all of which had had to be folded up because they were too long. 'He said to come informal; he actually said not to dress *down.*'

'What did he mean by that?' Delia enquired after a moment.

'It was a cheap and nasty shot at my dress if you really want to know—the one I wore last night. The one we agreed, you and I, was just right for making a statement at the Spences'.'

'Ah.'

'As you say,' Saffron agreed. 'So I decided to wear this tonight. You have to admit there's barely an inch of me visible and—'

'All *right*. Where did you get it?'

'It was my brother's,' Saffron said mischievously. 'I often wear it, incidentally. It's comfortable and—' she patted the pockets '—I can put all my pens et cetera where I can't lose them.'

'Saffron,' Delia glanced down at her smart black trousers and white linen blouse piped with black. She also touched her neat, straight brown hair which was tied back smoothly. 'Saffron, you must know very well that *this* address, the one on the packet,' she said dryly, 'is probably the very best there is here, and I feel bad enough about tagging along uninvited, but this—'

'I do,' Saffron said ingenuously, 'know what a

prestigious address it is! Always wondered who lived there as a matter of fact.'

'And you're still going to wear your old sand-shoes with that—that flying suit, and your hair fish-plaited as it's been all day?'

'Oh, yes, I am,' Saffron said. 'I told you it was informal. Shall we go?'

Delia muttered beneath her breath but Saffron laughed. 'I take full responsibility, Delia!'

It was a clear night as they drove the short distance from Saffron's golf-course condominium. There was a moon picking up the glitter of droplets on the fairways from the silent jets of the underground sprinkler system. The Hyatt Hotel was alive with lights, and the restaurants in the village were doing a brisk trade. The waters of the Coomera river lay smooth and glassy beneath the moon and reflected lights from the harbourside villas.

It was not a harbourside villa they drove to, however, but a riverside mansion with a high white wall on the road and impressive wrought-iron gates.

'Are you quite sure we should be doing this?' Delia said as she pulled up and wound down her window to speak into the intercom.

'Quite sure, Delia.'

'Miss Shaw and—er—Mrs Renfrew, sir.'

The dignified personage who had admitted them was unable to keep a slight note of disapproval out of her voice, and it seemed to echo down the huge room, with its stunningly simple decor and an entire wall of glass that overlooked the river. Most of the light came from outside, from round white glass lamps on the terrace, although there were a couple of lamps lit inside.

Fraser Ross was standing beside one pouring a drink, and he turned round with a slightly surprised look on his face.

Delia found herself wishing fervently that she could sink through the floor.

But Saffron surged forward in her impossible suit and said graciously, 'I *knew* you wouldn't mind if I brought Delia with me, Mr Ross. She's going to be very much involved in your project so I thought she might as well be in on the ground floor, so to speak.'

A deep chuckle came from further into the room and they all turned to see a silver-haired man.

He also said, 'Of course we don't mind. Do come and join me, Mrs Renfrew. I'm Bernard Ross. I have the feeling you got bulldozed into coming here tonight. Would I be mistaken?'

'My father, Mrs Renfrew,' Fraser murmured, and added, 'Please don't feel embarrassed; I quite understand.' And he led Delia over to the settee Bernard Ross occupied.

Saffron followed and said candidly to Fraser B. Ross, 'You're right, Mr Ross, sir. I did twist her arm a little. But then your son twisted my arm a great deal harder, which is why I'm here. How do you do, by the way? I'm Saffron Shaw.'

'Saffron,' Delia said beneath her breath.

'I'm delighted to meet you, Saffron Shaw,' Bernard Ross said. 'So he twisted your arm, eh? Thought something must have happened because I seem to remember being told quite distinctly that you were too busy for his house.'

'Yes. I was. Until he threatened to put me out of business. Didn't you?' she said cheerfully to Fraser A. as, without asking, he put a drink into her hand.

'*Saffron,*' Delia murmured again, and accepted a sherry with a ruefully apologetic little look.

'Don't worry, Mrs Renfrew,' Fraser the son said easily. 'What is going on could most aptly be described as "the games people play".'

'I hesitate to contradict you,' Saffron said blandly, 'but I never play games.'

'Put it this way, then—Saffron and I had a rather confrontational experience last night. She claims there was a misunderstanding involved. To which end I gather she has chosen to appear virtually in purdah tonight. Little to know,' he said with his head tilted thoughtfully as he studied Saffron, 'that purdah has its own appeal.'

There was a tense little silence, then another voice said, 'Darling, I thought you were looking for a *wife*!' And Diana Marr strolled into the light. She continued, 'Why, Saffron, *you* look like a boy tonight. What a metamorphosis.'

Saffron, in the act of seating herself, got up and drew herself to her full height. 'Why, Diana, how nice to see *you* again,' she said. 'And may I say you have set my mind at rest? On several scores. I quite thought your brother had designs on me and that's why he's blackmailed me into doing his house. But if he's *wife*-hunting, well, I don't need to worry, do I?'

There was utter silence. Then Fraser Ross said courteously, 'Dad, why don't you show Mrs Renfrew the water garden?' He leant forward and touched a switch on the wall and a panel of glass slid sideways, admitting the night air.

'Why not?' Bernard murmured, glancing at Delia, who rose.

Fraser turned to his sister and said equally courteously, 'Diana, would you tell Cook we need another place set for dinner? And please tell him we'll be ready in half an hour.'

'Half an hour! Why so long?' Diana objected.

'Saffron and I have some business to attend to first,' he replied mildly although there was a distinct quality of an iron fist in a velvet glove to it, Saffron thought, and raised her eyebrows.

Diana shrugged and walked away.

'And we'll go to the study, Saffron.'

'Will we?' she replied, studying his tall figure and noting that he was still dressed as he had been earlier in the day, then smiling coolly up at him. 'Perhaps I should first remind you that I'm not your sister or your father and I don't take kindly to being ordered around.'

'And perhaps I should bring it to your notice, Saffron, that you can either accompany me willingly or be picked up and carried there.'

'You wouldn't!' Her eyes were suddenly very green and distinctly stormy.

'I would,' he murmured, his dark gaze entirely mocking.

She glanced around, but Delia and Bernard Ross were out of sight, and so was Diana.

'I could scream!' she declared with a toss of her plait.

'That would certainly add a whole lot of undignified drama to the occasion,' he drawled. 'Don't you think you've been outrageous enough tonight as it is? Come.'

'You...I...I'm speechless,' she said furiously, but started to walk beside him as he put a hand on her elbow and directed her towards a doorway. 'You were the one who started all this. You're the one who thinks he can resort to the most despicable kind of blackmail and...and...'

'Ah, but whatever I've done, Saffron, has been done in private. I haven't embarrassed others—don't you think that's a little despicable?'

'No,' she said baldly as they walked down a passage and through another doorway. 'I happen to believe all's fair in love and war and I'm sure you do too so don't give me that!'

A door closed behind them and she realised they were in a study that looked over a tiled, lit courtyard with pretty statues, tubs of lovely flowering shrubs and trees, espaliered creepers and a delicate little fountain. 'By the way...' She swung round to face Fraser Ross with a question trembling on her lips that she didn't get the chance to ask.

Because he said, 'Love? I don't know about that but I've got the feeling there's only one way to shut you up, Saffron Shaw, and this is it.'

Saffron froze and her eyes widened as he walked towards her and took her in his arms.

'What do you think you're doing?' she demanded indignantly.

'What you hoped you might provoke me into doing when you put on this amazing outfit?' he suggested, glancing downwards with a slightly sardonic twist to his lips.

'I don't know what you're talking about—this is my brother's flying suit!'

'Is that a fact? And it didn't occur to you that if you were sensational last night, rather like an exquisite ivory figurine in a dress that was an invitation to undo, this—' he plucked the thick khaki twill with his long fingers '—is even more of an invitation?'

Her lips parted incredulously.

'I think the contrast would be rather stunning,' he murmured. 'The rough against the smooth. That silken skin, those delicious curves and satiny hollows, that—' he paused to glance down her body again then suddenly up into her eyes '—"do your damnedest" expression when you aren't wondering exactly what I'm wondering.'

'I…I…'

'Wondering in the case of last night, for example,' he continued with soft mockery, 'what it would be like if we were alone and the dress did come undone and start to slide down your beautiful body, Saffron. Correct me if I'm wrong, but I don't think you were wearing a bra so my first view would have been of high little breasts—probably pink-tipped and delicious—to taste and to touch.' He raised a dark eyebrow at her. 'Do you like to be—tasted?'

'Stop it; you're quite wrong!' She licked her lips. 'I wore this for the opposite reason. Well, because of what you said but also to discourage you completely if you *must* know.'

'Ah, but you left it too late, Saffron. The—damage had already been done, I'm afraid. I shall probably now always think of what was so nearly in view, what promised so much, whatever you wear.'

She took an incredulous breath. 'You really have to be the limit! And I refuse to participate in this kind of thing any longer—'

'See? I was right. About the only way to shut you up.' And he bent his head to kiss her.

Five minutes later, he looked down at her stunned expression and said wryly, 'You were about to ask me something, Saffron?'

CHAPTER THREE

'WH-WHO decorated this house?'

He laughed softly. 'As a regrouping of one's defences that's pretty good—I've no idea.'

Regrouping! Saffron thought a little wildly, and was not to know her face was pale, her eyes dark, her lips soft and pink. But she did know that during that kiss he'd sat down on the corner of the desk, and was still sitting on it with his hands linked about her waist, and that their eyes were level.

She was also on a level with everything about Fraser Ross that was so tormenting, for want of a better word. That hint, she suddenly thought, of swashbuckling piracy beneath the civilised exterior that seemed to go with his dark good looks and easy strength and made you imagine silly things. Such as being caught up, run off with and kept somewhere against your will by an amused, dangerously attractive captor.

She swallowed and blinked vigorously. 'How can you live in a house and not know that?' It was the first thing that came to mind to say and she licked her lips then said with more dignity, '*Would* you mind letting me—?'

'I don't live here. I stay here from time to time, that's all,' he interrupted quizzically.

'How come? Where do you live?'

'In Brisbane, although I spend a lot of time here,

there and everywhere.' He shrugged. 'This is my father's house,' he said with a fleeting grin, and removed his hands from her waist, but only to refold one of the sleeves of her flying suit that had rolled down over her hand. 'There.' He put his hands back around her waist.

'Look—'

'And he bought it as a "spec" home so it was already done. I take it you approve? Professionally?'

'Very much.' She considered. 'What I've seen, which hasn't been a lot, but—'

'Would you like a guided tour, Saffron? The bedrooms are beautiful.'

'You have an incredible nerve,' Saffron said in a low, taut voice at the same time as she tried to remove herself from his grasp.

A wicked little smile lit his eyes. 'And you have to admit there are times when we're not entirely unmoved by each other.'

'This is only the second time—' She stopped abruptly.

'We've been in each other's arms?'

'Yes. Will you let go?'

'Not yet,' he said easily. 'I'm afraid you're liable to claw me like an outraged kitten.'

'I wish you would stop calling me that!' she said exasperatedly. 'It makes me feel entirely ineffectual.'

His lips twisted. 'You weren't exactly ineffectual last night. Nor have you been a model of silence and discretion tonight. Although—' he raised an eyebrow at her '—I can't help admiring such spirit.'

'Can I tell you what I think?'

'I don't imagine there's much I can do to stop you

and I'm probably better off hearing it in private—be my guest.'

'I think you *need* a wife.'

He laughed, kissed her lightly on the lips, released her and stood up. 'You could be right. But until she comes along what's so wrong about you and I getting to know each other better?'

'This,' Saffron said through her teeth. 'I don't want to get to know you better, and if you mean going to bed with you why don't you come out and say it?' She gazed at him with magnificent scorn.

'All right. Why not?' He folded his arms and gazed back gravely.

'I'll tell you—I've sworn right off men, that's why.'

'That's strange,' he drawled. 'You didn't kiss me like someone who is sworn off men.'

'I didn't have much choice.'

'Now, Saffron,' he advised dryly, 'at least be honest.'

'Why should I be?' She frowned at the admission and felt her cheeks grow warm, but soldiered on. 'I haven't made any of the running, so to speak. Are *you* honest enough to admit that?'

'Perhaps,' he conceded although as if it slightly amused him. 'Tell me why you're sworn off men, then.'

'Oh, the old, sad story,' she said airily. 'Got my heart broken, don't trust the species any further than I can throw them—you know.'

He sat back on the corner of the desk and studied her. 'You seemed to be enjoying dancing with several of the species last night before I came along.'

'They weren't men, they were only grown-up boys.'

His lips twitched. 'Really?'

'Yes. You see,' she confided, 'I can pick them a mile off—the ones I can handle. They generally turn out to be quite fun, good for a bit of escorting when the need arises, good to dance with, but that's about it.'

'What was his name?'

Her eyes darkened. 'None of your business.'

'I see.'

'What do you see?' She tilted her chin at him.

He stood up again, rolled her other sleeve up, patted the collar of her flying suit into place and restored a stray tendril of hair to its rightful place beside her ear.

'Would you mind not handling me without my permission?' she said crossly because he had somehow reduced her to feeling about fifteen, amongst other things. '*What* do you see?' she added with a fighting little glint in her eyes.

'I thought for a moment you were having me on, Saffron. I see now that you weren't. But it's not only childish to invest the whole tribe of men with the sins of one of us, it's probably not good for you either. In other words, you might not be such a termagant if you—'

As slaps in the face went, it wasn't terribly successful. Her sleeve unravelled again and got in the way. What it earned her in return was a considerable loss of dignity.

He took both her wrists in one hand, and laughed down at her. He also said, 'Don't you think you should find someone your own size before you attempt physical violence, Miss Shaw?'

'If you mean am I afraid you'll retaliate,' she spat, 'no, I'm not!'

He raised his eyebrows. 'You really shouldn't be so sure of that, Saffron. You may be quite safe with me, but others...' He shook his head wryly. 'And there are different ways and means of retaliation, you know,' he added softly, his dark eyes scanning the way the front of her flying suit was moving in tune with her accelerated breathing.

Quite sure she was about to be kissed again, Saffron drew her resources together and said with a not entirely assumed little air of world-weariness, 'Oh, not that, Mr Ross. If you mean the kind of retaliation I think you mean—getting yourself kissed for a slap in other words—how boringly banal!'

'Perhaps I was right earlier—would you rather I tore your clothes off and made love to you on the floor?' he suggested evenly.

A sudden imp of mischief lit her green eyes as she thought, Aha! Not quite so amused any longer, are we, Fraser A. Ross?

'You suggested it, not me,' she murmured, and the imp got out of control and she had to laugh.

What he would have done was destined not to be known because a knock came on the study door, and the disapproving personage who had let Saffron and Delia in put her grey head around it to say, 'Dinner is served, Mr Ross.'

'Ah, Flora.' Fraser Ross released Saffron's wrists. 'Sorry, I didn't introduce you earlier, but Flora is re-

sponsible for my correspondence when I'm here—
Saffron Shaw, Flora MacTavish.'

'Oh, so you…' Saffron bit her tongue and advanced
to offer her hand instead.

Flora MacTavish put her head to one side, looked
severely at Saffron, then, amazingly, said, 'I like the
cut of your jib, young lady. Come and have dinner.
Cook has been known to throw the odd tantrum when
he's been kept waiting.'

Dinner was delicious—a delicate, pale green soup
with cream twirled artistically through it, an entrée of
smoked salmon, a main dish of chicken Maryland and
a sinfully sumptuous chocolate and ice cream dessert.

The dining room—the *small* dining room, Diana
had made a point of telling them—had a terracotta
tiled floor, green walls, white cane furniture, pottery
tubs of yellow chrysanthemums and several paintings
on the walls that Saffron would have sold her soul to
own.

Indeed, Saffron enjoyed not only her surroundings
but also every bit of her dinner, to the surprise of
some.

'You have an amazingly large appetite for a small
person,' Diana said.

'There's nothing wrong with that,' Flora, who obviously enjoyed almost familial status, countered with
a tinge of aggression. 'There's more to life than wor-
rying about one's figure.'

Saffron, in the act of spooning up the last of her
ice cream, put down her spoon. But Delia spoke for
her.

'Saffron burns up an enormous amount of energy,'

she said. 'There are times when I find it hard to keep up. Besides, she often forgets to eat.'

'I've noticed that,' Fraser Ross murmured. 'The excess of energy, I mean.'

'Would you mind not discussing me as if I was some sort of *enfant terrible*?' Saffron said irritably as her dessert plate was removed and a coffee cup was put in its place.

Bernard Ross chuckled. 'An unusually attractive one if that's the case, may I say, Saffron? And I find your outfit entirely original.'

'Do you?' Diana queried with a raised eyebrow. 'I was wondering whether it came from a second-hand shop.'

'Saffron,' Delia put in hastily, 'why don't you show us the sketches you made this afternoon, and tell us about some of your ideas. They're rather wonderful, I think.'

Saffron paused in the act of shooting Diana an old-fashioned look and patted her pockets. One of which yielded a small sketch book that she studied for a moment, then her expression cleared and she tore the top sketch off and handed it to Bernard Ross. 'I have this vision...' she began.

'So that's how it's done,' Fraser Ross murmured to Delia several minutes later as they watched Saffron and Bernard deep in conversation as Saffron delivered her ideas.

'Never fails,' Delia replied softly. 'She's fallen in love with your holiday house, by the way. I just hope you approve of a Javanese influence because that's what you're going to get.'

He raised a wry eyebrow.

*   *   *

'Saffron?'

Saffron roused herself as Delia drove them home. 'Mmm?'

'Despite your worst efforts that didn't go off too badly, did it?'

My worst efforts? Saffron thought. 'No.'

'And you do have to see the place, don't you?'

'Yes.'

'I know tomorrow morning isn't that far away but I can hold the fort for a few days, I promise. Are you—worried about not having the right clothes for flying off to the Whitsundays at such short notice?' Delia asked patiently.

Saffron glanced at her witheringly.

'Thought not. So what is it? They *liked* your ideas. He's paying all your expenses including first-class air fares and first-class accommodation on Hamilton Island—'

'All right, I'll tell you, Delia,' Saffron said frustratedly. 'The man…reminds me of a pirate!'

'A…?' Delia turned into Saffron's driveway.

'A swashbuckling, devil-may-care buccaneer. I can quite easily picture him carting me off on his galleon or whatever pirates use and—having his way with me!'

Delia switched the motor off and stared at her. 'Saffron, I know you have a wonderful imagination, but isn't that a little—far-fetched? I would say he's very civilised, very adult and so on.'

'He's never kissed *you*, Delia,' Saffron replied frostily.

'Kissed…? When did he do this?'

'Never mind, Delia.' Saffron straightened and tilted

her chin. 'Would you do me a favour? Would you drive me to the shop? If I'm going to do this there's a lot I need to do beforehand. I'll walk home when I'm finished.'

'But—'

'Please?'

Saffron didn't get home until two o'clock in the morning, and remembered she still had to pack. But she had a shower first, donned a dark green towelling robe and made herself a cup of herbal tea. She took the tea into her bedroom, pulled down a travel bag, then sat on the end of the bed with a sigh. To think darkly of how she had been literally press-ganged, although so, so civilly, into this trip up to the Whitsundays the next day—*today*, she amended.

The fact that the next few days were the only few days that Fraser Ross could see his way clear to be flying up to his holiday home in the near future had been mentioned first. The fact that it would not be possible to get to his island unless she was unusually handy with motor boats had been made known to her when she'd suggested that she didn't need *him*, only his house.

Whereupon she'd had to admit that, although she loved sailing, she'd never driven a motor boat in her life. Then it had been brought home to her politely, but with an underlying glint of mockery in those dark eyes, that she was the one who had stipulated a time limit...

That was when she'd stiffened her spine, flashed him a look that had told him to go to hell, and announced to all and sundry that he needn't think she would renege on her business obligations so, if there was nothing else for it, she would go.

She pulled some pins out of her hair, unplaited it, lay back flat on the bed and closed her eyes. But that didn't stop Fraser Ross's image from swimming behind her eyelids. Nor did it banish the memory of the way he'd kissed her. And the way she'd so far forgotten herself as to respond.

What is it about him? she wondered desolately. He couldn't be physically more different from Simon, whom I loved with every fibre of my being, I thought. So it's not that I'm reminded... He's also the last kind of man I would dream of getting involved with. Powerful and prepared to use that power to get his own way. Apparently looking for a wife, but prepared to dally along the way—there's obviously no chance of me being considered wife material for the Ross family.

She sat up abruptly and wondered if she was going mad to even be thinking along those lines. But none of it changed the fact that...it was exciting to be in his arms. It curiously and treacherously interfered with her better judgement and brought out an answering chord of sensuality.

She touched her lips involuntarily and recalled all too well the smooth, powerful feel of him, the way they'd looked into each other's eyes—she with hostility, he with cool irony—and how it had further charged the air between them to produce a passionate little encounter that had been rather stunning in its intensity.

I must be mad, she mused. Is this the result of all work and no real play for so long? Or is it simpler?

Don't most women have a secret hankering to play with fire at least once? Because I'm pretty sure that's what it would be.

She sighed again and got up to pack, muttering to herself as she did so. '*One* dress for dinner, a couple of pairs of shorts and shirts, night gear, undies and, oh, well, perhaps a swimsuit! That's all I'm taking, Mr Ross.'

'Travelling light, Saffron?' Fraser Ross said casually when she came out of her front door the next morning to see him sitting behind the wheel of a dark green Mercedes convertible with the hood down.

'Yep.' She tossed her bag into the back seat but put her briefcase down with more care. She wore jeans, a cream blouse, short boots with thick soles, and she slung a navy blazer into the back as well. 'And if you make one remark about my clothes or lack of them I'm liable to bite,' she warned.

What she received in return was an enigmatic dark glance and some barbed little comments. 'You brought it up. Has it been bothering you? Interfering with your sleep?' And, when she ground her teeth, he laughed and merely advised her not to be silly and recommended that she get in.

She slid into the front seat beside him and immediately requested that he put the hood up.

'Why? It's a lovely morning.'

'It may be but I didn't bring a scarf. I'd refuse to be seen dead in one anyway, but I have the kind of curly hair that responds to the breeze in a way that makes me look like a mop.'

'Ah.' He glanced at her hair, lying loose and natural. 'Or is this your way of telling me you're not at all impressed?'

'Probably that too. If you must know I find it terribly ostentatious.' She looked around at the acres of light tan leather. 'I'm surprised you're game to leave it in an airport car park.'

'I'm not. Someone is coming to pick it up at the airport.' He touched a button and the roof slid up and over. 'I gather you're not in a good mood this morning, Saffron?' He drove off.

'Never am when I've had my arm twisted.'

'Why don't you think of all the dollars about to flow in? And the exposure?' he suggested blandly.

She shrugged. 'We didn't get around to discussing brass tacks. Of that kind.'

'We could discuss it now.'

But Saffron sighed suddenly and slid down in the seat.

He glanced at her. 'What's wrong?'

'Tired, that's all. Because I worked last night after we left you,' she said pointedly. She considered a little bleakly and shrugged. 'And I'm prone to bitchiness as a result. Sorry.'

'This is a little surprising, Saffron.'

'It's also a temporary state of affairs, no doubt.'

'No doubt. Why don't you have a little kip?'

'I may not be able to help myself,' she murmured, and her eyes closed. Two minutes later she was fast asleep.

Once or twice, Fraser Ross glanced at her as the big car purred up the Pacific Highway towards Brisbane airport, but she didn't stir. She slept neatly, he thought, and—his lips twisted—with the kind of wholeheartedness with which she did everything. He caught himself wondering about her background, and the man who had broken her heart. Then he paused to wonder why he'd gone to the lengths he had to secure her services for his holiday home.

He shrugged with a slight frown in his eyes. She'd certainly been eye-catchingly desirable as the belle of the ball two nights ago. Then it had come as something of a surprise to discover that this sprite in her mid-twenties, this slip of a girl, had been responsible for the formal little note of rejection he'd received. And to have Diana warning him off, so to speak, had obviously added a little spice to it all.

Spice, he repeated to himself as he stopped at the Gateway Bridge toll booth, but Saffron slept on. And he wondered with a touch of dryness whether that meant he was jaded and disenchanted. With women, in other words, who made it abundantly plain that they would regard it as an honour to be Mrs Fraser A. Ross, and would accord the position their all, especially when it came to spending his money.

He drove the last few miles to the airport, feeling distinctly disenchanted but at the same time quite sure that a spitting little cat of a girl, however desirable she could look, with, moreover, a definitely one-track mind, was not the answer. So why *was* he doing this?

'Have I offended you?' Saffron glanced at Fraser Ross.

'No. Why do you ask?'

They sat side by side in the broad, comfortable first-class seats of the jet that was winging its way up the Queensland coast to Hamilton Island in the

Whitsunday group of islands, so named by Captain Cook in 1770 for obvious reasons.

'You don't seem your usual urbane, sometimes affable self,' she said with a tiny smile. 'Was it me falling asleep? I am sorry.'

'And you are all refreshed and geared up to resume hostilities as you promised, I gather?'

Saffron looked affronted. 'I've just apologised.'

'At the same time as you used words such as "urbane" and "affable"—with every intent to needle me.'

Saffron widened her eyes then had to laugh. 'Yes,' she confessed. 'I don't suppose I'd like to be described as urbane and affable, but I really didn't think I'd—wound you with them.'

'Well, now you know.'

'I see. But I thought you were rather quiet *before* I called you urbane and affable.' She eyed him curiously.

He looked up as the stewardess brought their lunch trays. She was a groomed and glossy girl who was obviously not unaware of the attractiveness of at least one of her first-class passengers, judging by the amount of attention she'd lavished on Fraser A. Ross. And he glinted a charming little smile up at her before she moved away.

'Perhaps you'd rather be sitting next to her?' Saffron suggested sweetly as she unwound her cutlery from its napkin. 'Perhaps she's overnighting on Hamilton—now there's a thought.'

'Attempting to procure for me, Saffron?'

'Attempting to dispel the gloom,' she said with a shrug.

'Does that mean to say you're viewing this previously *despised* commission with more enthusiasm?' He looked at her dryly.

Saffron considered as she ate some delicious asparagus vinaigrette. Then she wiped her mouth, contemplated the next course, and said, 'I was very hungry, to be honest. So food, especially first-class food, has induced a general spirit of *joie de vivre* in me. Didn't have time for breakfast in other words,' she added laconically.

'Remind me to add that to my list of tips,' he murmured.

'Tips?' She frowned at him.

He looked wry. 'On how to handle Saffron Shaw.'

'You...have a list?'

'I'm acquiring one.'

'May one ask where from?' Her eyes glinted dangerously.

'Well, personal experience has contributed most of it,' he replied agreeably. 'Feed you, keep your mind on your work—and, if all else fails, kiss you.' He looked at her blandly.

Saffron choked on a mouthful of delicious beef in burgundy sauce.

'Have a sip of wine,' he recommended.

She did so, but her eyes were still watering as she glared at him.

'Not quite so full of the *joie de vivre* any longer, Saffron?' he queried with a faintly malicious little smile.

She took a deep breath, and suddenly decided against further hostile remarks. For the simple reason that she didn't doubt Fraser Ross was spoiling for a fight and, in this mood, might just win it. 'Not really. I've never been to the Whitsundays,' she confided with an ingenuous little smile, 'so there's that to look forward to. No. I'm still feeling pretty happy with life at the moment.'

For a moment his expression defied description then he chuckled softly. 'You're full of surprises, Saffron.'

'I know,' she agreed. 'That's why I'm so successful.'

'Your modesty is also overwhelming.'

'Oh, I can be modest. Not, generally, when it comes to my work, though.' She finished her lunch and patted her stomach. 'That was pretty good.'

'Glad you approved.' This time, he didn't smile at the stewardess when she removed their trays, topped up their wine and poured their coffee. He merely inclined his head.

It was left to Saffron to notice the slightly crestfallen look in the girl's eyes. 'Wise,' she commented. 'She was definitely getting her hopes up.'

'And you feel this is your business, Saffron?' he said with a tinge of irony.

'Directly? No. Indirectly, don't forget I side with your sister.'

'I didn't think you and Diana would find much to side about at all.'

'You have a short memory.' Saffron eyed him mockingly then remembered her earlier resolution. She sighed theatrically. 'No, you're right; it is none of my business.' But she couldn't help adding, 'You're supposed to be looking for a wife, that's all.'

'Wives can come—from all walks of life.'

'Of course.'

But something in the way she said it caused him to look at her sharply. And to say, 'Spit it out, Saffron.'

She shrugged. 'I would imagine, when you're very rich, the problem is to sort the wheat from the chaff. Those that want you, those that want your money. Mind you, you have a lot of other things going for you; that I do concede.'

'How kind.'

She grinned. 'Perhaps we should change the subject?'

He stretched his long legs. 'All right. Tell me about your background. We have about twenty minutes before we land.'

'Oh, it won't take that long. My father is an artist, my mother was a—very minor—opera singer. They're divorced—have been for years—they're both remarried now with new families, they live at opposite ends of the continent and, although they were thoroughly unsatisfactory as parents, they're rather nice.'

'And you have no brothers and sisters?'

'I have a twin brother. We don't look very much alike.'

'Ah. The pilot?'

'Yes. He's in the air force based at Amberley at the moment. I'm actually the elder by about half an hour.'

'So that accounts for the independence? As well as the flying suit.'

'Being half an hour older? I doubt it, although…'

Saffron stopped and looked rueful. 'He claims I have a tendency to boss him around.'

'I can imagine. No. I meant having divorced parents.'

'Oh, that—probably.'

'And such a fierce determination to succeed?' he asked after a moment.

'I might have been born that way but what really fostered it was…' she hesitated then said colourlessly, 'Something else.'

He glanced at her. 'What?'

'Well, I think that's the end of show-and-tell, Mr Ross. We're coming in to land.' She did up her seat belt.

'Something to do with the man who broke your heart?' he hazarded, with a narrow look at her shuttered expression.

'No.'

'I don't believe you, Saffron.'

'If you think—*All right*,' she said through her teeth. 'He not only broke my heart—which is ridiculous; of course he didn't!—but at the same time he managed to…undermine my confidence. He wasn't the sort of man who took easily to having a successful woman by his side. And he actually got me to the stage of believing I didn't have what it takes.'

'This is a man you believed you loved?' he queried sceptically.

'Put it this way,' Saffron said grimly. 'This was the man who alerted me to the awful problem men have with their egos. This was also a man…with a lot of money.'

'Oh, I see,' Fraser Ross said softly. Then he remarked, 'We've landed. Welcome to the Whitsundays, Saffron.'

An hour later she was sitting in a smart little motor launch, which was nosing its way out of Hamilton harbour.

She'd changed into shorts and a T-shirt but otherwise had barely had time to draw a breath, let alone take in a great deal about Hamilton Island except to note that her room in the tall Hamilton Towers was cool, spacious and very comfortable. The other thing she had noted was the heat, and she wished suddenly that she'd thought to throw in a hat.

They cleared the entrance leads and Fraser Ross opened up the throttle. He'd also changed into shorts and a T-shirt.

'How far?' she yelled above the roar of the powerful outboard.

'Ten minutes. You're not scared of boats, are you?'

'I shouldn't be, I've crawled around enough of them and I do know a bit about sailing— Gosh!' She looked around wide-eyed. 'This is rather lovely.'

The water was a clear turquoise and the spray they were raising was silver. There were islands all around them—some big, green and bare, others small and thickly wooded—all, apart from Hamilton, apparently uninhabited. But there was also the heat and the clear air and it suddenly came home to her that she was in the Great Barrier Reef Marine Park, in the tropics, and that it would be lovely to spend a holiday here.

Fraser grinned down at her as she drank it all in then took off his peaked cap and handed it to her. 'Be careful of the sun!'

*   *   *

Ten minutes later, she said in an awed voice, 'This…is your very own island?'

'I have a very long lease. That's how things work here.'

Saffron stepped over the front of the boat and jumped down onto soft sand. Fraser Ross's island wasn't large; in fact it was a perfect little jewel in this shimmering water wonderland. Then she frowned. 'But I can't see a house and there's no jetty. How do you get things brought here?'

'By barge,' he answered. 'The house is there—' he pointed upwards '—if you know what to look for between the trees.'

'I love those trees.' She narrowed her eyes. 'What are they?'

'Hoop pines—not to be confused with Norfolk pines although they look rather similar. Come.'

He held out a hand and she took it after a moment. They climbed a steep little path through the bush and, suddenly, the house was there in front of them.

Saffron stopped and blinked. Because it couldn't have been more perfectly done, and even the photos hadn't done it justice. Fashioned out of what she knew enough to know was western red cedar that had weathered to a silvery grey, it sat on its niche on the hillside surrounded by the tall dark green hoop pines as if it had grown there. It flowed with the contours of the island and brought a smile of sheer satisfaction to Saffron's lips.

'Shall we go inside?' Fraser suggested.

'Yes. Can I ask you a favour, though?'

'Why not?'

'Would you mind not talking to me? First impressions are terribly important,' she said seriously.

'Won't say a word,' he promised.

She broke the self-imposed silence once.

'There's nothing here.'

They were in the kitchen that was rather reminiscent of a ship's galley in that it was compact and functional, but with wonderful, hard-wearing Corian benchtops that cried out for some of the innovative Italian-designed stainless-steel appliances she'd seen recently. But there was no refrigerator, no stove, no dishwasher, and the drawers and cupboards were empty—as was the rest of the house.

'No,' he agreed. 'That's where you come in, isn't it?'

'You mean you want me to furnish it down to the last teaspoon?' She looked at him wide-eyed. 'Everything?'

'Every last thing. Pots, pans, brooms, towels and sheets, beds, a stove, the lot. What else is there? Is that asking too much?' He eyed her quizzically.

'Oh, no. It's a designer's dream, not to mention a woman's dream,' she said unguardedly. 'I just wasn't expecting quite...' She paused.

'Such a free hand?' he suggested. He was leaning back against a counter with his arms folded, watching her curiously.

Saffron grimaced, irritated to think just how much amusement she afforded Fraser Ross. She said tartly, in consequence, 'I just hope a wife doesn't pop up out of the blue, Mr Ross. You might find that wives have their own ideas when it comes to pots and pans, that they like to choose their own crockery and the colour of their sheets.'

'There doesn't appear to be any danger of that happening in the near future, Saffron,' he murmured wickedly. 'So why don't you put yourself in the place of any future wife I may acquire? A wife by proxy kind of thing.'

Saffron bit her lip and eyed him coolly. 'Are you having a go at me?'

He raised his eyebrows at her. 'Now why would I be doing that?'

'Nothing you did would surprise me greatly,' she replied frostily. 'But two thoughts came to mind. That what you said was a jibe at my decision to be a businesswoman rather than a wife, and that it might be a bid to get me thinking along the lines that so obviously occupy your mind extensively.'

'Such as?' he asked softly.

'Getting me into your bed, as if you didn't know,' she retorted.

He laughed and straightened. 'Possibly. But you were the one who brought wives up, Saffron. Could that indicate a *subliminal* line of thought?' His gaze roamed over her as she stood so taut and ready to fight him every inch of the way in the middle of his empty kitchen.

But Saffron was beginning to see the trap yawning at her feet, and she backed away verbally. 'No, only a practical line of thought,' she countered evenly. 'Still, when one is as wealthy as you are, I don't suppose it matters. You can chuck out the things she doesn't like and start again. Would you mind getting out of my way?'

'Before you—punch me or something like that?' he suggested gravely.

'Not at all. So I can measure up for a fridge and a stove. And would you mind not talking again?'

But her mood of aggression subsided as, with camera and tape measure in hand, she moved around the house. She also used a small tape recorder to talk her impressions into.

And finally she packed them away and said to him with a sigh, 'It is lovely. You're very lucky, and I have to confess it will be a bit of a joy to work on it. I don't often get the opportunity to do things from absolute scratch. You can take me back now.'

CHAPTER FOUR

BACK in her room on Hamilton, Saffron immediately plugged in the laptop computer she'd brought with her and made copious notes on it. And she was pre-occupied as she changed for dinner.

She showered, washed her hair and sat on her ve-randah as the sun set and lights started to twinkle on the island. Then, as a deep violet dusk hid the waters of the Whitsundays, she went back into her room to put on her only dress.

It was white, a pique cotton, with a halter neck and a low back, and was three-quarter length. She slid her feet into a pair of black patent sandals, tied her hair back in a bunch and put on a pair of huge gold hoop earrings. She'd just applied a bronzey lipstick when there was a knock on the door.

'Coming,' she called, and made herself concentrate on her appearance. Only to be suddenly reminded of another dress that hadn't required a bra. But while her sea-green gown had had a stiffened, boned bodice this one didn't. She turned sideways and tried to see her back in the mirror, then turned to the front and stared at herself minutely. It wasn't see-through, she de-cided, but it was pretty obvious there was no bra be-neath it.

Damn, she muttered to herself, why don't I stop to think? Then, with a little shrug, she went to answer the door.

Fraser, dressed in khaki trousers and a checked shirt, was waiting patiently, leaning over the half wall of the passage, looking into the night. He turned and straightened.

'Will this do?' Saffron asked. 'It's all I brought.'

He looked her over with a wryly lifted eyebrow.

'What's that supposed to mean?' she queried with her chin tilted.

'That you'll do, that's all,' he said mildly. 'There's a restaurant on the beach, thought we'd eat there. We can sit outside and watch the moon.'

'How nice,' she replied, just a shade dryly.

They walked through the main complex with its soaring ceilings, across the bridge over the huge swimming pool lit from underwater and up the steps to his chosen venue for dinner.

The Beach Bar and Grill struck Saffron as Polynesian-inspired. It was pleasantly casual, with a nice island atmosphere to its timber construction, and the smell of good food abounded. Fraser got them a table on the verandah, ordered steaks for both of them, and a bottle of wine. A laden table groaned beneath a delicious self-service selection of salads, vegetables, desserts and breads.

But Saffron was more interested, it seemed, in the moon and the way it was lightening the sky so that the bulk of Passage Peak was just visible across the beach and bay.

So much so that as they ate their steaks she barely said a word and appeared to toy with her food.

Finally, Fraser pushed his plate away, poured himself another glass of wine and said, 'Saffron, I'm seriously worried.'

She drew her gaze to him and blinked. 'Why?'

'Well, you asked me not to talk while you got your first impressions of the house, but I didn't realise it was to last all evening. And you're not eating, which, from the way I've seen you enjoy your food, is a little ominous.'

'Oh, that.' She grinned ruefully. 'Sorry. It's very nice, the food, but I've got—' she wrinkled her nose '—something on my mind.'

'Such as?'

She was silent as she finally finished her meal and picked up her wineglass. Then she said with a little sigh, 'Zanzibar.'

'Zanzibar. Did I hear right?' he asked after a moment.

'Mmm... The thing is, nice as your front door is, what your house really needs is a set of Zanzibari front doors. Only I can't work out how to get my hands on them.'

'A Zanzibari front door?' he said seriously, then started to laugh. 'Look, why don't we start from the beginning—have you ever been to Zanzibar?'

'Of course I have!' Her eyes were large and indignant. 'Would I suggest—?'

'All right.' He raised a pacifying hand. 'But you have to admit it's not a common destination from this part of the world. It's not somewhere we pop off to for a little break.'

'Perhaps not,' she conceded. 'But you don't have to make it sound as if I've been to the moon and back.'

'Sorry. Well, then, tell me about these front doors.'

Saffron sat forward eagerly. 'They're incredible. I

don't know if you realise, but Zanzibar—which is the quintessential spice island—also has a long history of association with the sultans of Muscat and Oman.'

'My knowledge of Zanzibar is quite limited,' he confessed.

'OK. Well, they ruled the island for a while, into this century as a matter of fact, hence the significant Arab influences. One of them is their carved and brass-studded front doors.'

'I see.'

'Now, the purpose of them harks back to ancient times when the longish pointed studs served to repel invaders on elephants—to stop the elephants from simply pushing down the front door of your house in other words. Not that that was actually ever a problem on Zanzibar—I don't think they had elephants there— but all the same...'

'This is fascinating,' Fraser said. 'I hesitate to point it out but we don't have elephants here either.'

'Of course we don't,' she said impatiently. 'But these doors are an art form. So, incidentally, are the marvellous Arab chests inlaid with brass and the four-poster Zanzibari beds that they make there.'

'And you seriously feel my house would not be complete without them?'

Saffron drank some wine and regarded him thoughtfully for some time. Then she said coolly, 'Look here, Mr Ross. The reason, I presume, that you sought my services in the first place was because my ideas are original?'

'True.'

'So I take it you don't want your house to look like any other old house?' she pursued relentlessly.

A faint smile twisted his lips. 'No—'

'And, so far as the doors go, did you or did you not mention that security is the reason why you don't have a jetty—could be a problem in other words? If an elephant couldn't break down your front door, a mere mortal definitely couldn't.'

'True again. But I hadn't envisaged paying your fare all the way to Zanzibar, Saffron, in order to be a bit different and provide security.'

'Which is exactly why I'm a bit preoccupied,' Saffron shot back triumphantly. 'Of course I don't expect you to pay my fare to Zanzibar As a matter of fact it's the last place I want to go, lovely as it is.'

'So?' He stared at her quizzically.

'I have two options. I have the name of a supplier in Zanzibar, but that could take months. Or I could try to find someone here to replicate them, but—' she shook her head '—I'd really rather have the original.'

'I thought you were going for a Javanese influence.'

'Oh, I still am. But they'd complement each other wonderfully.'

'Very well.' He topped up her wine. 'I'll tell you what to do. Get me a quote for a set of front doors and a chest, all genuine. Also a delivery date. I'll make a decision then.'

'And a bed?'

'No,' he said definitely. 'When it comes to beds I prefer to be very conventional—and comfortable.'

She chuckled suddenly. 'Actually, although they're very picturesque, they weren't that comfortable—not the ones we…I slept in, anyway.'

He watched the glow leave her face and the way

she sat, tense suddenly in her pretty white dress. Tense, beautiful in her rather uncommon way, and slightly tortured, he thought, and decided to try a shot in the dark. 'He was in Zanzibar with you?'

'Who?' She looked at him through her lashes.

'The man who so turned you off men, Saffron. Or have there been a series of them?'

'Oh, dozens,' she replied flippantly but with a steely little glint in her eyes.

'You don't lie very well,' he said after a taut moment.

'Look at it this way—how many women have you had, Mr Ross? And, while we're about it, why don't you tell me how your taste in women runs? We could have a lovely long discussion on that subject, I'm sure!'

'You're telling me to mind my own business, I gather,' he said amusedly.

'Yes, I am.' She looked away moodily.

'Well, then, would you like a walk along the beach?'

Surprise then suspicion held her silent as their gazes clashed.

'Or you could do it on your own, Saffron,' he said softly. 'It really doesn't matter one way or the other to me.'

'I...I might go straight to my room,' she answered stiffly. 'I'd like to ring Delia and ask her to fax details of my Zanzibar contact immediately, and I want to sort out some other ideas I have as well. By the way, I do appreciate you making that decision so promptly. People who can't make up their minds drive me mad.'

'I can imagine,' he said dryly.

'Well, goodnight. Thank you for dinner.' She stood up beneath his oddly dispassionate gaze, then sat back down abruptly to say irritably, 'How do you do it?'

He raised an uninterested eyebrow at her.

'Make me feel guilty and—churlish! OK! I'll walk along the beach with you on one condition.'

'That I don't kiss you?'

'Precisely.'

'Funny, I had that on my mind as well,' he murmured, then laughed outright at her expression. 'I'm suitably warned off, however.' He stood up. 'Let's go.'

They walked to the end of the beach companionably.

Fraser told her a bit about the Whitsundays and Hamilton Island as they went, and they stopped once just to drink in the magic of the night and the moon. The tide was high and left a tracery of silver on the beach as it lapped the sand.

It was then that Saffron turned to make some comment to him only to have it die on her lips as she was gripped by a feeling that was a little hard to handle, in view of her express conditions governing this walk.

But the fact of the matter was, it was suddenly impossible to be unmoved by Fraser Ross, standing tall and relaxed beside her with his dark hair lying on his forehead, his hands shoved into his pockets and his shirt blowing slightly in the breeze.

And she felt her nerve-ends tingle and her senses long for the magic of how it had felt to be in his arms that first night. She remembered the clean, starchy smell of his shirt and the pure man beneath it. She remembered his hands on her body, the feel of her

body against his, and was plagued by a sudden surge
of sheer desire.

She remembered, in intimate detail, their kiss of
the next night and how she'd wanted to run her hands
through his hair even while she'd hated herself for
it... She drew her gaze away from him and stared out
to sea. But that didn't help because her imagination
took wings and she remembered her pirate fantasy,
helped along by this place, these lovely waters, and
how—magical it would be to be sailed away with
from here.

'Saffron? Is something wrong?'

'Oh! No. Why?'

He looked down at her and she caught her breath
and only just stopped herself from saying. Is it the
same for you, Fraser? Are you *really* as attracted as
I...seem to be?

'You look a little stunned.'

'Sorry. I was thinking, that's all.'

'Not about some more exotic things for my house
such as Zanzibari doors, I hope,' he said wryly.

She managed to give a husky little laugh, and
started to walk again. 'Probably, but I shall desist.'

'You can tell me,' he said on a different note, and
she went hot and cold because she was suddenly sure
he had guessed that her thoughts were far from
Zanzibari doors.

But that was when she came to grief. She caught
the toe of her sandal in a vine coming down from the
grass verge beside the beach, and she tripped and fell
awkwardly.

'What is it?' he asked as he helped her up and
heard her suddenly indrawn breath.

'My ankle; I sort of twisted it as I went down, I think.' She clung to his arm and put her foot down gingerly only to gasp in pain.

'Sit down; let's see.'

'No—'

'Saffron, do as you're told,' he ordered, and bodily picked her up to sit her down on the grass. He gently manoeuvred her foot, causing her to gasp again. 'You've sprained it, I'd say. Let's get you back to your room then we'll call the nurse.'

'I'm *sure* we don't need to—'

'Shut up, Saffron,' he advised. 'Look, can you hobble on it now? I'll help. And do me a favour—don't talk. After all, I did as much for you this afternoon.'

An hour later, Saffron was sitting on her bed propped up by pillows with her swollen ankle neatly strapped and resting on another pillow. The nurse had just left and had been of the opinion that it was a sprain, not a break, but that Saffron should stay off it as much as possible in the next couple of days. She'd left some painkillers.

'Thanks.' Saffron looked up and accepted a cup of coffee from Fraser. Her hair had come loose, her earrings were on the bedside table, and she looked a bit pale but also wry.

'I know what you're going to say.' He pulled up an armchair and sat down beside the bed. 'You should have stuck to your original plan.'

'Yes. Never mind; it could have been worse, I guess.'

He looked at her enquiringly.

'I could have broken it, I suppose.'

'Yes.'

'All the same—' she heaved a sigh and put her hands up to ease the knot of her halter neck '—it's going to interfere with everything. I wanted to go back tomorrow and take more measurements, reinforce some of my ideas. It is a perfect nuisance, actually.'

'You took a lot of measurements today. You also took your own photos. And window measurements et cetera are on the plans.'

Saffron propped her chin in her hand. 'Mmm… You know, another thought I had was no curtains. Blinds, louvres and shutters—what do you think?'

He looked thoughtful and wondered if she realised that the easing of her halter had not stopped her dress from outlining her obviously braless breasts in all their small, firm and pointed perfection.

Or realised that cynicism, disenchantment or whatever the hell it was that had led him down this path had not made him any less aware of her and that lithe, lovely body, nor stilled the growing curiosity in him about just how she would make love. With the passionate intensity she did most things?

'They're not only visually perfect for a house like that, but they don't fade, sag or blow about,' she said seriously.

'Makes sense,' he commented. 'I'd still like to see some more sketches, now you've seen the place in the flesh, so to speak.' For some reason this seemed to amuse him.

'Of course. Uh—' She frowned at him.

'What now, Saffron?' Has she guessed what is oc-

cupying my mind much more than curtains or the lack
of them? he mused.

'I'm wondering...' She paused. 'Just how to im-
print some of your personality on the place. I don't
want you to feel as if this is simply a show place—
or is that what it's to be?'

'At times,' he agreed after a moment, and with a
wryly lifted eyebrow, then sought to become serious.
'I thought you enjoyed the thought of being able to
do everything from scratch.'

'I do,' she said frustratedly. 'But...' She stopped.
'Oh, well. So it is to be a bit of a show place but not
entirely?'

'Yes. I have a few business interests in this part of
the world. I'm selling this part of the world tourism-
wise in other words. But I also intend to—relax here
from time to time.'

'And what do you do when you relax?'

'Eat, drink, sleep, swim, fish, go boating. I'm pretty
normal in most respects. What did you think?' There
was a tinge of sardonic amusement in the way he
returned her look.

'I thought you'd make a pretty good pirate if you
really want to know.'

He stared at her and noted how the sudden colour
stained her cheeks. 'Seriously, Saffron? In what respect?'

She bit her lip and cursed her impetuous tongue.

'A pirate when it comes to women?' he suggested
softly but with the most devilish little glint in his eyes.

She tried to shrug offhandedly. 'You have to admit
you've shown some pirate-like tendencies in regard
to me.'

'So you're living in constant dread that I might sweep you up and make off with you?'

'Not at all,' she said haughtily and with a slight disregard for the truth. 'You wouldn't find it that easy to kidnap me.'

'True. Unless, in your heart of hearts, you wouldn't mind a little of...that kind of excitement?'

Saffron blinked several times and wondered how to refute this rather close-to-the-bone allegation. Drat him, she thought hotly. And how did I get myself into this? She eventually said tartly, 'Don't you wish, Mr Ross.'

He considered her quizzically. 'Perhaps it's what you need, Saffron. To get you over what was apparently a disastrous affair.'

'Like a hole in the head,' she denied vigorously.

'Do you still love him?' he asked curiously.

Saffron hunched her shoulders and stared at her cup. And, to her amazement and absolute horror, two tears slid down her cheeks. She dashed them away and said impatiently, 'It's over. Why do you keep—?' She stopped abruptly.

'Because I'm just wondering, *if* you do, whether success and a career are going to compensate for it.'

'It's not that,' she said after an age. 'It's, well, the waste, I guess. Of emotion, time, self-esteem.'

'That's one thing you don't seem to lack.'

She lifted her head and, although her eyelashes were wet and spiky, no more tears fell. 'Good,' she said briskly. 'I'm glad you think so. Can we get back to your house?'

He put his cup down on the bedside table and stood up. 'I've got a better idea. It's been a big day; I think you should go to sleep. It is also ten o'clock, Saffron,' he added as she opened her mouth to protest. 'Do you need a hand?'

'No. No, thank you,' she amended more graciously.

'Well, if you do I'm next door and you can ring me. Goodnight. Don't even think about working, by the way. It'll all keep until tomorrow.'

'I—' But she changed her mind at the look in his eyes, and was amazed to hear herself saying meekly, 'All right. Goodnight.'

It wasn't a good night, though.

Her ankle ached and her dreams were threaded with images of a past love and a new attraction, if that was what it was.

Of course it is, to an extent, she told herself wearily as she lay in the dark wide awake at one stage. You wouldn't be thinking of things such as the way he picked you up and carried you up the stairs to the lift as if you were a feather otherwise. You wouldn't remember the feel of his arms, how nice it was to lay your head on his shoulder, the little quickening of your pulses when he put you down but kept you close...

You wouldn't have come so close to giving yourself away on the beach or experienced the forbidden thought that wouldn't stay forbidden, and the tremor of excitement it brought—that it would be nice to be going to the same room, the same bed.

And all this from someone who firmly disbelieved in casual sex, prided herself on it, and genuinely believed her first relationship would lead to marriage?

Saffron, Saffron, she chided herself. Don't let this get out of hand!

She fell asleep again eventually, to be woken by the sound of a key in her door. And, in procession, came Fraser Ross, a waiter pushing a trolley and a bellboy pushing a wheelchair. There was also bright sunlight flooding the room.

Saffron sat up, pushed the hair out of her eyes then pulled the sheet up hurriedly, her green satin nightgown only having shoestring straps and a rather revealing neckline.

If anyone noticed, they didn't betray it by so much as a twitch of a muscle.

'What—?' she began.

'Morning, Saffron,' Fraser said amiably. 'Brought you breakfast. How are you?'

'Fine, but—'

'And here it is, ma'am,' the waiter enthused, pushing the trolley right up beside the bed and removing covers from the plates. 'If there's anything else you'd like, please call us. *Bon appétit!*' He left, ushering the bellboy out.

'I could have come to breakfast' Saffron protested.

'Then you left it a little late.'

She stared at him owlishly.

'It's ten-thirty.'

She lay back then sat up almost immediately. 'It can't be. I never sleep in.'

He came to the bed and showed her his watch. 'Would you like to freshen up first?'

'I—thanks.' She accepted the matching satin robe that had been lying across the bottom of the bed and struggled into it. Then she got out of bed and hopped awkwardly to the bathroom where she washed her face and brushed her hair, and wished heartily that she didn't have an audience waiting for her.

She said as much as she hopped back and sank down into the chair he'd pulled up to the trolley. 'I'm not at my best first thing in the morning.'

'Who is?' he responded with a grin. 'But I was beginning to worry.'

Saffron grimaced and tackled a small fruit platter as well as downing a glass of orange juice. Then she chose some wholemeal toast from the bread basket and buttered it, and took in his appearance. He wore white shorts, a sky-blue T-shirt, white canvas loafers and his thick hair was damp. He also looked fresh, penetratingly alert and almost too much of a fine physical specimen to bear—if you had only just got up yourself and somewhat precipitately at that.

'I suppose you've been up and about for hours?' She pulled a delicious-looking ham and tomato omelette towards her.

'Long enough to have a game of tennis and a swim before I had my own breakfast.'

Saffron looked interested. 'Who did you play with?'

'I happen to know the coach at the Racquet Club. He put together a set of mixed doubles.'

'Mixed?' She raised an eyebrow at him.

'Yes. Funnily enough with two stewardesses, one of whom you went out of your way to warn me off, Saffron.'

'Aha! What a small world it is!' Saffron continued to eat her omelette imperturbably.

He laughed and pulled up a chair opposite her.

'You're so right. May I pour your coffee? I ordered some for myself.'

'Thanks.' She pushed her plate away. 'I was starving.'

'I believe you,' he murmured. 'May I also bring these fine blueberry muffins to your notice?' He unfolded a linen napkin.

'No, thanks,' she responded ruefully. 'I'm not really a glutton. So—how did she play?'

'Well enough. We won.'

'And did you get an opportunity to inspect her for her wifely qualities?'

'No. Don't be bitchy, Saffron.' His eyes glinted with satire.

She drew a breath but relented suddenly. 'OK, I won't say another word on the subject! By the way, there's no way on earth I am going to allow you to trundle me around in a wheelchair,' she added as her gaze fell on the offending object. 'I was actually wondering whether we shouldn't try to go home today.' She eyed him seriously.

'Not a chance.'

'What do you mean?' Her seriousness turned to irritation.

'I don't feel like going home today,' he replied easily. 'I want to go over to the house again for one thing. As for the wheelchair, there's no reason why you shouldn't enjoy a bit of this wonderful, tropical sunshine, have a swim in the pool and relax today. Of course I could always carry you about. Is that what you'd prefer?'

Saffron shot him a dark look. '*No*. I could also stay here—'

'How is your ankle feeling?' he interrupted. 'Perhaps it's up to walking on properly. Why don't you give me a demonstration? Your earlier ones weren't very convincing.'

She bit her lip and glared at him.

'Then don't argue, Saffron.' He stood up. 'I've never met such a shrew. I'll be back in half an hour to take you down to the pool.'

It took her a while to recover from the 'shrew' remark but on the whole she enjoyed her sojourn down at the pool—at least the first part of it.

The sun was lovely, the sound of the sea was soothing, the loungers were comfortable. And Fraser Ross helped her to repair some of the deficiencies in her packing. He wheeled her first to the shopping mall where she bought a hat, some sunscreen, a pair of sunglasses, and on impulse a gauzy shirt to wear over her bikini instead of the T-shirt she had on. She also purchased a book to read, and then, to carry it all, a raffia bag.

'Do you always have to do this along the way?' he queried with a grin as he wheeled her to the pool.

'I wasn't really thinking of holidaying,' she replied.

'Well.' He lifted her effortlessly out of the chair and put her gently down on a lounger. 'You look like the complete holiday-maker now, albeit a wheelchair-bound one.'

She grimaced, stuck the peaked cap on her head, donned the sunglasses, picked up her book, and chuckled suddenly. 'You're so right!'

He sat down next to her and stripped off his shirt. 'Why not do the same?' he suggested casually.

Saffron hesitated and looked down at her T-shirt. 'When I warm up.'

'OK.' He lay back and closed his eyes. 'Give me a call when you feel like a swim.'

'Do you often do this?' she asked about ten minutes later.

He opened one eye. 'Do what?'

'Get comatose in the sun?'

'No. Not often enough,' he answered ruefully. 'Why? Aren't you enjoying it?'

'Yes, but…' She hesitated. 'Not as much as you, obviously. You know—' she sat up and crossed her legs '—no one would take you for a millionaire madly busy businessman at the moment.' She eyed him curiously.

'What do you think they'd take me for?'

'I'm not sure,' she answered slowly. 'It's quite difficult to put you against a background, Fraser. I don't suppose I've ever seen you in executive mode, for one thing. I've never seen you at home, for another.'

'Homes haven't ever been terribly important, I guess,' he said after a slight pause. 'But I live in an apartment on the south bank of the Brisbane river, if that helps at all.'

'Oh! That sounds nice. You mean those blocks close to Southbank and the Lyric theatre? The art gallery?'

'The same. And, if I may pre-empt you, I have no idea who decorated it. It was another "spec" deal.'

Saffron chuckled. 'You're a lost cause in some respects, aren't you?'

He sat up and she took a slightly unsteady breath at the way his muscles flowed beneath the tanned skin of his shoulders and back. 'I thought I was remedying that by hiring you, Saffron.'

'That's true,' she conceded. 'I hadn't thought of it quite like that, but—'

'So there's hope for me yet?' He looked at her with a wicked kind of gravity.

She grimaced and sighed.

'What now?'

'Nothing! Well...' She shrugged and looked around.

'You're champing at the bit to get back to work,' he filled in resignedly.

'No, not really, but I suppose I do find it hard to relax.'

'The book's no good?'

'I don't know,' she confessed sadly. 'I just can't seem to get into it.'

'Then we'd better have that swim now. Perhaps you need to be tired out a bit before you can relax.'

Saffron heaved a sigh then sat up determinedly and shed her hat and her shirt. 'I can—' she began, swinging her legs over the lounger. But she got no further as he scooped her up and carried her into the pool.

And the sheer shock of the cooler water temperature made her cling to him as well as gasp as he sank them both beneath the surface up to their chins.

'Only way to go,' he murmured, his eyes wicked and laughing. 'Getting in by degrees prolongs the torture, don't you agree, Saffron?'

Her teeth chattered. 'You're a sadist, Fraser Ross!'

'No, I'm not.' He lay on his back and punted them through the water gently. 'It's not that cold; it's just that you'd got pretty hot, body temperature-wise. Can you swim?'

'Of course I can swim.' But for some reason she didn't pull free. For some reason her body, in its pretty but scanty pink, green and white floral bikini, seemed loath to leave the security of his arms, the nice feeling of closeness and the way her skin felt satiny and so smooth against his.

'Saffron?' he said gravely. 'Not entertaining any of those pirate thoughts?'

Her eyes locked with his, and perhaps he saw the little flare of shock in the depths of hers that was tantamount to an admission because he resisted her sudden attempt to break free.

'There's nothing especially terrible about it, is there?' he said softly at the same time. 'We're actually consenting adults, not captor and captive.'

She twisted out of his arms this time, but he caught her around the waist and advised, 'Go slowly, my little wildcat. It's always best to be honest, you know. Think what happened to you on the beach last night.' He drew her closer, so their bodies were touching under the water.

'How…I wish you *wouldn't*,' she said exasperatedly, then stopped frustratedly.

'Wouldn't read your mind?' he hazarded softly, and moved his hands down to the neat, taut little curves of her buttocks. 'Perhaps it's because we're so often of the same mind? Such as right now. Such as…' he paused and looked wickedly into her wide, fixed gaze '…how much I would like to peel this bikini bottom off your lovely, jaunty little hips, and how much you would like me to. So tell me, what would be so wrong about it, Saffron?'

Her lips parted and her slender body moved beneath his hands, but the moment was broken by someone swimming up to them, calling his name gaily. Someone Saffron recognised even out of her smart stewardess uniform.

'Everything,' she said through her teeth, and pulled away successfully.

CHAPTER FIVE

SAFFRON elected to have lunch in her room.

She had in fact swum quite a few lengths of the pool, revelling in the freedom of movement after the restrictions her ankle placed on her on land, then simply floated in what was actually a heavenly temperature as the heat of the day built up.

It had become quite a lively party around the pool, with both stewardesses and the tennis coach joining them. Fraser had ordered long, cool, exotic drinks, and plans for lunch and the afternoon had been made.

The tennis coach—a friendly man called Bob of about the same age as Fraser and obviously an old friend, had made it known it was his afternoon off. The stewardesses, Gloria and Cathy—Cathy was the one Saffron remembered from the flight—had made it known they would be happy to be included in any activities at all.

And Fraser had invited them all to accompany him to his island that afternoon. Cathy had also, in a rather delicate aside, sought to establish just what the relationship was between Saffron and Fraser at one point.

'Oh, I'm only his interior decorator,' Saffron had replied, and added with no delicacy at all, 'Please don't hold back on account of me.'

Unfortunately, a lull in the convivialities had caused this remark to be audible to all. Cathy had blushed and Fraser had allowed a suddenly hard, dark glance to play over Saffron. She, on the other hand, had lain back on her lounger unaffectedly, and closed her eyes to the sun.

And that was when things had broken up, ostensibly so they could all get ready for lunch, and Fraser had wheeled her back to her room.

'Thanks,' she said briefly as the door closed behind them, and got out of the wheelchair, only to have her ankle collapse beneath her. She muttered beneath her breath and staggered to the bed.

'I'm almost tempted to say serves you right, Saffron,' Fraser Ross drawled as he came to stand in front of her.

'For *what*?'

'For being as recalcitrant as only you can be,' he said softly but with a dangerous glitter in his eyes.

'I'm not being recalcitrant,' she denied coldly. 'I'm being honest if anything. And I've told you once before, I don't play games. I'm here to work and work I shall.'

'You're also spitting with jealousy, Saffron.'

Her face was already pale from the pain of her ankle, but it paled further at this. She made a huge effort, however, to contain herself. 'Think what you like,' she said casually. 'And by all means go ahead and enjoy yourself this afternoon. I can't join in even if I wanted to; it's quite simple.'

'But you don't want to either?'

'No. I'm perfectly happy to spend the afternoon preparing some more sketches. It's really time we got down to brass tacks, Mr Ross,' she said formally. 'I'll need your approval to go ahead now and place some orders.'

He regarded her as she sat on the bed in her new blouse with her fists plonked beside her and the light of battle, although latent, in her eyes. 'All right,' he said mildly. 'What about lunch?'

'I'll order it to be sent up here.'

'That mightn't be a bad idea,' he observed thoughtfully.

'I'm glad you approve, but why?' she couldn't help answering.

'I have the feeling you're just dying for the opportunity to be even more recalcitrant.'

'The recalcitrant decorator? Dear me! Why—?'

'No, the reluctant lover, Saffron. OK, have fun; I'll check in some time this evening.' He swung on his heel and walked out.

Saffron stared towards the doorway for several minutes then lay back on the bed and felt thoroughly at odds with herself.

But a few moments later she got up and made a phone call to Delia, and received something of a surprise at the end of it. Delia, it transpired, had been invited to have dinner with Bernard Ross that night.

'Why?'

'Well...' Delia hesitated down the line '...he's just asked me, that's all. We...yesterday he asked me out to lunch, then we went to the movies, and had dinner too.'

Saffron blinked several times as this sank in, and made some quick calculations. Bernard Ross would be about sixty, she judged, and was distinguished-looking, and, not only that, nice. Could it be possible...?

'Look, have a lovely evening,' she said warmly

because her very real affection for Delia made her long to see her find happiness.

All the same as she put the phone down her mind was buzzing. How would Diana react to a step-mother? How would Fraser? Just let them do anything to upset Delia, she thought hotly, then had to smile weakly. It was only a dinner date...

She shrugged and resolutely turned to work.

She had only one interruption during the afternoon.

The nurse came up to see her, bringing an ice pack and an elasticised ankle guard.

'Mr Ross rang me to say you were still in quite a lot of pain,' she revealed. 'These should help. I also brought a walking stick I managed to lay my hands on. By tomorrow you might be able to use it instead of being pushed around.'

'Oh, thank you,' Saffron said with real gratitude. 'I do hate being pushed around.'

At six o'clock she sat back with some satisfaction at the final sketches of the main entertaining areas of Fraser Ross's holiday home plus plenty of notes.

She yawned and decided to have a shower. It was dark by the time she was dressed again in shorts and a T-shirt and she sat on the verandah, staring out to a sea she couldn't see. And feeling—she couldn't deny it—lonely and sad. Not that she wanted to be taking part in any of the partying she had no doubt would be planned for the evening, but for the first time for several years she didn't want to be alone...

You fool, she thought. He's not for you and you're not for him. If you had any sense, the last thing you'd be doing would be prolonging the matter by getting carried away over Zanzibari doors. He is a man women flock after; he can take his pick, and I'm sure he does.

But she sat like that for another ten minutes, unable to shake her mood. Then there was a tap on the door and she steeled herself to ignore it, but it opened and she realised the nurse must have neglected to lock it when she'd left. She turned cautiously, knowing it would be him but unable to see until a lamp sprang on.

'Saffron?'

'I...I'm here.' She swallowed.

He wore the same khaki trousers and checked shirt that he had the night before and he looked bronzed from the sun, dark, tall and terrifyingly attractive. He paused then walked to the verandah doorway. 'All right?'

'Yes. Fine, thanks.' But it came out more huskily than normal.

He narrowed his eyes and watched her for a moment—the way she sat, deliberately upright, the cloud of russet curls framing her small face, her hands clenched in her lap, her unconsciously rigid expression. Then he grimaced and pulled up a chair to sit down beside her. 'Did you get the ice pack?'

'Oh, yes. It...I...it was very thoughtful of you. How was your afternoon?'

'Nice.' He reached over, prised her hands apart, and took one in his. 'How was yours?'

'Very productive,' she said after a moment. 'It's all set out there on the table, but we can go over it tomorrow.'

'We can go over it now if you like.'

'No. You're probably on your way to dinner—'

'I'm not.'

'And— What did you say?'

'I'm not on my way anywhere. I have no plans for this evening, in other words.'

Saffron's lips parted and she searched his eyes. 'But I thought...' She stopped confusedly.

'You thought Bob and I had set ourselves up with a couple of willing birds?' he suggested.

'Well...' She looked embarrassed and licked her lips. 'I...suppose so.'

He smiled briefly. 'So I gathered. But it *was* pure coincidence that I met up with Gloria and Cathy this morning. And it was...' He paused, thought a little wryly about certain words he'd uttered on the subject of honesty earlier, and continued, 'Pure malice that prompted me to organise the outing this afternoon.'

'Malice?' Saffron repeated, her eyes wide and very green.

'I'm afraid so.' He looked down at her hand in his. 'Directed squarely at you, Saffron.' He raised his eyes to hers and they were wry.

'M-me...me?' Her voice stuck in her throat.

'Yes, you. My enormous ego got dented once again.'

'Because I...?' She couldn't go on.

'Because you were so determined to resist even my most friendly impulses. Would you like a drink?'

She blinked rapidly. 'Uh—yes, thanks.'

He got up and went over to the minibar. 'A glass of wine?'

She nodded.

He came back with wine for her and a beer for himself. 'And all the while you were working away, thoroughly enjoying yourself, no doubt,' he said softly as he pulled the ring-top and poured the beer into a glass.

Saffron took a sudden and urgent sip of her wine. 'I did do a lot of work, yes. I also spoke to Delia. You may not believe this but your father is taking her out to dinner this evening.' She stopped abruptly, aware that she was babbling and that she'd had no intention of telling Fraser Ross that anyway.

'Ah. I thought that might be on the cards. He was rather taken with your Mrs Renfrew.'

'I see. Well...' She took a breath and thought, Seeing that I started this I might as well say my piece. 'I have to tell you that Delia has been badly hurt once and I wouldn't be at all happy to see her getting hurt again.' She stared at him defiantly.

'Saffron...' He stopped, looked at her exasperatedly then laughed. 'Two things,' he said at length. 'I'm not my father's keeper, but *he's* not the type who deliberately goes around breaking hearts, believe me. Neither of us is if it comes to that. I know you have that opinion of me but it's not a very accurate one.'

'How did you—?' Again she stopped abruptly.

'How did I guess? It wasn't hard,' he said.

Saffron stared into her wine, speechless for once in her life. It didn't last for long. 'You did—' she looked up into his eyes '—you *did* blackmail me into this.' She sought for the right words and produced ones that made him smile slightly. 'If I've been difficult it hasn't been without cause.'

'I have yet to seduce you, however,' he said a

shade dryly. And as her eyes widened he added, 'Did you honestly think I would put you out of business, Saffron?'

Her mouth fell open. 'Yes. Well. It wasn't entirely why I—agreed, but, yes, I did!'

'I hesitate to ask this but why *did* you agree?'

'I...' She paused, frowned then said, downbeat, 'I couldn't resist showing you I could fight back, I suppose.'

'How?' he asked simply.

A bleak little shadow touched her eyes. 'If you don't know, don't ask. I'm renowned for my retaliatory instincts, most of the time. So it's only been a game for you?'

'Not entirely. Does it feel like a game when you're in my arms?'

She coloured and looked away.

'Tell you what,' he said after a moment, 'why don't we try to make a fresh start? Why don't I order dinner? Are you hungry?'

'I'm starving,' she said sadly.

'All right—seriously starving? What happened to lunch?'

'I forgot about it.'

'I might have known. You need a keeper, Saffron Shaw! Why don't I order dinner to be sent up here, and we could go over all your hard work of this afternoon at the same time?'

Saffron sat as still as a statue for a moment, then she brightened visibly. 'Yes, please.'

'Is there any...? I'm still a bit worried that this will turn into a show home, not a real home,' she said perplexedly a couple of hours later. 'I don't really like to work that way. Are there any of your own things you'd like me to know about? You see, in the matter of homes, it's actually easier to work with a woman. Even Mrs Whitney Spence had some favourite pieces she wanted me to work around.'

They had dined sumptuously. Fresh, delicious oysters to start with then grilled fish for Saffron and roast beef for Fraser. Dessert had been a pavlova stuffed with strawberries and topped with whipped cream.

'Sarah had some ideas of her own?' Fraser got up to push the trolley with the remains of their meal away and pour their coffee.

'Some ghastly ones. I don't know if you saw the bedrooms, but Josephine would never have lost Napoleon if she'd had Sarah's bedroom,' Saffron said with a shrug. 'I very much regret that house, you know.'

'I wouldn't. A lot of people thought it was wonderful. I see—' he flipped through some sketches '—you've been very restrained with my bedrooms.'

'Yes. I decided not to set myself up as a proxy wife in that regard. I also thought that the climate up here,' she continued swiftly, 'didn't lend itself to too much frippery.'

'So, simple, masculine but comfortable,' he murmured.

'Is…is it all right?'

'In case I decide to share it with a female person on the odd occasion?' His gaze was wicked.

'A bed is a bed is a bed, and I promise I'll get you the most comfortable and spacious one I can find,' Saffron replied dryly. 'But to get back to what we were discussing.' She sat forward intently. 'I want you to feel this is a home. I think you're discerning enough to know the difference.'

He studied her thoughtfully.

'I mean, even men must know what they like and feel comfortable with,' she added.

He gestured to the sketches. 'I think these exhibit both comfort and style. I'm happy with them, Saffron. You can go ahead with my approval.'

She sat back feeling curiously let down but couldn't exactly pinpoint why. Then, out of the blue, it occurred to her that what she really wanted to know was more about the man. She bit her lip as this hit her as well as the realisation that it wasn't precisely out of the blue, this desire. She picked up her coffee cup.

'Saffron?' He looked at her with a raised eyebrow.

'I...it's nothing. When will we go home?'

'Tomorrow if you like. Unless you'd like to take one more look at the place. By tomorrow your ankle could be a lot better.'

'No. Um...no. If you are happy, there's no need.'

'So why do I get the feeling you're not?' he asked after a short pause.

She put her cup down and stared at the tablecloth, then she looked up directly into his eyes. 'This...couldn't work.'

He sat back and watched her narrowly. 'I gather you're talking about us?'

'Yes.'

The silence lengthened as he thought to himself, You're probably right. But what is it about you, Saffron Shaw, that makes me determined to keep trying? Those soft, severe lips that I've plundered so pleasurably? That lovely, heavy hair, the apparently unquenchable spirit? The fact that you're one of the very few who's ever said no...?

'Tell me why you think it couldn't work,' he said at last.

She formed her hands into a steeple and he saw the concentration in her green eyes, which made him want to laugh yet was curiously endearing.

She said quietly, 'I could never fit into your lifestyle. I've been accused of being hyperactive for one thing. I would never consider letting my business go after all the work it took to get to this stage and—' she shrugged '—I'm just not the kind of wife I could visualise for you.'

'Aren't we jumping the gun a little?'

'Well, that's the other thing. I'm not built for speculative affairs.'

'That's very moral, Saffron, and—'

'Don't patronise me, Fraser,' she warned with a little glint of anger.

'Sorry,' he murmured with a twist of his lips. 'Tell me about the kind of wife you visualise for me, then.'

She stared at him steadily then said frustratedly, 'I don't *know* you that well.'

'But you must have formed some opinions to make a statement like that.'

She bit her lip then thought for the second time that night, In for a penny in for a pound! 'Working on the fact that you appear to be *looking* for a wife, the fact that your sister is concerned that you find one soon—and, of course, the *right* kind of wife—'

'My sister would be the last person I'd consult, Saffron,' he said dryly.

'All the same, I can't help thinking that the position requires someone with a suitable background—someone with the skills to fit into your very wealthy lifestyle, someone who is a good hostess, very decorative, beautifully presented, very discreet, intelligent and above all an asset to the house of Ross—but not necessarily someone you love madly.'

There was a dangerous little pause, then he said, 'Go on.'

'I don't fit into a lot of those categories.'

'You're intelligent and can be very decorative,' he said with a suddenly wry look.

'Only when I want to be. And I'm far from discreet, the only kind of hostessing I like to do is the impromptu kind, I don't give a damn about the Ross empire, I—'

'Saffron.' He held up a hand, and there was open laughter in his eyes now. 'Spare me.'

'Can I say one more thing, though? I will anyway. I think loving you would be a bit of a heartache. I don't think it would be easy to get through to the real you at all; I think it would be like hitting your head against a brick wall.' She paused. 'I think too many women falling all over themselves to get both you and your millions might have left their mark—left you somewhat cynical,' she said very quietly.

His dark eyes narrowed. Then he said with a tinge of savage impatience, 'You may think you know me better than you do, Saffron.'

She shrugged and rubbed her face wearily suddenly. 'Sorry. But I can't help it if those are the vibes I get.'

'You're sure you're not basing all this on your obviously vivid imagination?'

'Yes. I'm in fact basing it on this—you tell me now it was only a game to threaten to put me out of business. I can't help thinking that only a man who is dangerously bored with women would go to those lengths. And I can't help knowing that I have neither the time nor the inclination to play those kind of dangerous games with you.'

'So what do you suggest we do? Kiss and part company?' he drawled.

'No, stick to strictly business, Fraser,' she returned evenly.

'You think that's possible?' His gaze was sardonic. 'Is that why you were sitting in the dark feeling all lost and forlorn until I arrived? Or—'

She got up unsteadily and reached for the walking stick. 'I—'

'No, answer me, Saffron,' he said roughly. 'Were you or weren't you?'

'The times I happen to feel sorry for myself have nothing to do with you,' she shot back.

He stood up and removed the walking stick from her grasp. 'And are you very sure you're not convicting me of wanting the kind of wife a certain lover of yours tried to mould you into?'

Her eyes widened.

'Tell me about him, Saffron,' he commanded, and picked her up to sit down in an armchair with her in his lap. 'No, don't bother to struggle and fight,' he added. 'You're wasting your time.'

Saffron subsided with a little pant of pure frustration. But, although she ceased to struggle physically, she said bitterly, 'That's the other thing—you do carry on like a pirate at times.'

A sudden smile tugged at his lips. 'You're enough to bring out those tendencies in any man. But let's not sidestep the issue. You've made yourself very free with all sorts of wild assumptions about me, but I intend to get to the bottom of you. How old were you when this disastrous affair started?'

She stared at him mutinously until he said dangerously, 'Saffron…'

'All right! Twenty-one.'

'How long did it go on for?'

'Six months.'

'How did you meet?'

She blinked and sniffed. 'I was re-covering the upholstery on his boat, his fifty-six-foot yacht. You may not know this but that's how I got started.'

'Go on.'

She sighed. 'He was thirty. We fell in love. I think he did genuinely fall in love with me. He taught me to sail, and we seemed to like a lot of the same things. I'd always wanted to travel to out-of-the-way places; so did he.'

'Hence Zanzibar?'

'Yes.' She grimaced. 'It was like a voyage of discovery. At the same time, it's when the rot started to set in. He asked me to marry him there, one moonlit night at a place called Lala Salama, which translates approximately to "sleep peacefully". It was beautiful, white beaches, a reef, palm-thatched rondavels. I said yes. He said—' she swallowed '"—Then as soon

as we get home you can give up work and devote
yourself to me.'''

'And that's when reality hit?'

'Yes. But I should have known sooner. He never
took what I did seriously although he took his own
work very seriously.'

'What was he?'

'A doctor. But his family are very wealthy pasto-
ralists. To give him his due, they're also very conventional—or old-fashioned. His mother and his
brother's wives make an absolute virtue of domestic-
ity—always being there for the children, always putting their men first.'

'We're not talking about Simon Harris, are we?'

Saffron twisted her head to see him frowning down
at her. 'Do you know him?'

'Yes. Well, I know the family. You poor kid,' he
said with unexpected compassion. 'They're famous
for their stiff-necked ways.'

Saffron sniffed.

'So you refused?' Fraser suggested.

'I tried to reason with him first. I told him that
nothing could get in the way of how much I loved
him, but I couldn't just sit at home and paint water-
colours. I told him… Oh, well.' She moved restlessly.

'Tell me.'

'I…it ended eventually with him throwing things
up at me—such as it wasn't as if I was going to make
a successful career out of making seat covers, whereas
his career was a genuine calling and he'd need my
wholehearted support. That he had more than enough
money to support us anyway and…' She stopped and

sighed. 'He was—is—a wonderful doctor, and perhaps I was a fool.'

He ran a hand through her hair. 'You were only twenty-one.'

'I'm only twenty-five now,' she said unhappily.

'But amazingly successful! Think of that.'

She laughed a husky little laugh and sighed. 'So I am.' And she sniffed again.

'Here.' He pulled a hanky out of his pocket and handed it to her. 'You were also more of a realist than he was, Saffron. You did the right thing.'

'Thanks.' She wiped her eyes and blew her nose.

'And there's been no one since?'

'No. If nothing else, you must see now that I'm not built to take these things lightly.'

'Yes,' he agreed.

'So, getting back to what started all this, it couldn't work.'

He was silent.

'Fraser?' she said at last.

'Are you expecting me to argue with you, Saffron?' Again he stroked her hair.

She flinched inwardly. 'Of course not. Just to understand. I do like you, you see—when I'm not hating you, that is. Does that make sense? Probably not, but—'

He laughed. 'Perfect sense, for you. All right, I accept defeat.'

'Thanks,' she murmured, but made no move to get up. In fact, the awful truth of it was that she was not in the least thankful, she discovered. She was as lonely and sad as she had been earlier, or would be, once he left.

'Saffron?' he said gently, and turned her face up to his.

'I…I…' she stammered. 'I don't know what's wrong with me.'

'Perhaps I can tell you,' he said quietly, his gaze taking in the confusion in her eyes, the uncertainty of her expression. 'As masterly a summing-up as that all was, it still ignored one basic fact. There is a certain way that we like each other very much, but it's a way that's notoriously resistant to plain common sense.'

'I…you're right,' she said barely audibly. 'I don't know what to do.'

A strange expression flickered through his eyes. 'Yes, you do,' he said after a moment. 'Get up and walk away, Saffron. I'm no seducer of unwilling girls but I am human.'

She sat up. '*You* were the one who put me here!' But she stopped abruptly and her cheeks flamed. 'All right,' she muttered, and got up off his lap. 'I'm sorry. I…that wasn't fair.'

He lay back and studied her with some irony as she clutched the edge of the table then his lips twisted wryly and he stood up himself. 'Goodnight. I'll book us on the ten-thirty flight tomorrow. If I were you I'd just go to bed. Although why don't you dream about your next project? That guest house with twenty-five different bedrooms. It might help.'

He ruffled her hair with a careless hand, and left.

Saffron got ready for bed in a troubled daze. And, knowing she'd have trouble sleeping she took some time to prepare herself meticulously. She brushed her hair and tied it back with a green ribbon. She cleansed her face, put some moisturiser on, then, thinking of her exposure to the sun that morning, she moisturised herself from top to toe and finally arrayed herself in her emerald-green satin nightgown.

She also got into bed, turned off the light and tried to banish her woes by determinedly calling to mind the guest house. But it was no use. So she sat up, switched the lamp on and picked up the book she'd bought that morning. That proved to be an even worse idea, however. It was a love story, and some demon of perversity, after she'd read a chapter, made her flip through to the last couple of pages to discover that it ended happily.

Some demon of sheer frustration then caused her to hurl the offending book across the room. And she lay back on the pillows with her arms folded across the sheet and thought, *All right*! Have it out with yourself, Saffron Shaw.

Fraser Ross intrigues you and excites you. He has done from almost the first moment, but to contemplate going to bed with the man is sheer madness. Your masterly summing-up was pretty close to the mark; after all, he didn't try too hard to deny it. So...

She jumped as the phone beside the bed rang. It was Delia.

'Delia! Is something wrong? You frightened the life out of me. It's...eleven o'clock.'

'Saffron, I'm trying to get hold of Fraser. His father has had a heart attack— Look, they think it's a very mild one, but all the same—'

'Oh, no! While you were having dinner?'

'Yes,' Delia said, distraught. 'I thought he was going to die, but he isn't.' She swallowed audibly.

'Well, so far as they can tell. But he keeps asking for
Fraser. And the switchboard up there has tried his
room but there's no response. I wondered if you
might know where he is.'

'Well…' Saffron paused and her eyes darkened.
'Um…I might. Uh…give me the number you're calling from and I'll get back to you as soon as I can.'

She put the phone down a few moments later, her
thoughts in a chaotic whirl. If Fraser wasn't in his
room, did it mean he was with someone else? Such
as Cathy? Who, she had no doubt, would welcome
him with open arms.

But I don't even know her surname, and how embarrassing to have to knock them up if I did she
thought agitatedly. But, hang on, didn't she mention
she was on the same floor, only a couple of doors
down? Didn't I see her key this morning? Yes! Four
doors down to be precise. Oh, this is awful—and how
like a man!

It was the last thought that propelled her out of bed
in a mood of extreme militancy. She flung on her
robe, grabbed the walking stick and hobbled to the
door.

She'd just got out into the passage and was heading
towards Fraser's door when a distinctly sardonic
voice spoke behind her. A voice she recognised only
too well—Fraser…

'Changed your mind, Saffron?'

CHAPTER SIX

SAFFRON whirled around and all but fell over.

Fraser strolled up to her and steadied her but with that clear, mocking little question repeated in his eyes as they drifted down her figure in its featherlight coating of green satin—the décolleté neckline, the way the sash of the robe accentuated her tiny waist, the way one shoulder of the robe was slipping down, revealing the shoestring strap beneath, a pearly shoulder and the swell of her breast.

'Where have you been?' she demanded, going hot with embarrassment and plucking her robe closed to her throat.

'For a walk. Checking up on me, Saffron?'

She coloured vividly this time. 'No! Of course I'm not! That is…'

'I'm afraid the way you're blushing tells its own tale,' he drawled, and touched her hot cheek. 'You weren't—' he paused and frowned '—hoping to catch me in Cathy's arms, by any chance?'

'No, I was not! That is…how dare you?' she said in a low, angry voice.

'Then what the hell are you doing out here in your sensual and rather revealing nightwear?' he countered in a suddenly hard voice. 'And what the hell are you looking so guilty about?'

It shot through Saffron's mind that she was in an impossible situation, and placed there by her own

111

hand, more or less. It also occurred to her that she hated him for drawing the conclusions he had, for all the wrong reasons, but couldn't deny at the same time that he'd also caused her to feel extremely guilty.

She drew a quivering breath and said tonelessly, 'I did wonder if you were with Cathy. Sorry, but—'

'So you decided to catch us in the act?'

'*No!* Look—'

'Saffron—'

'Fraser Ross, if you don't shut up,' Saffron said dangerously, 'I'll do it for you! I am *not* a voyeur; I was not seeking you out because I'd changed my mind but because—' She hesitated suddenly and sighed. 'I'm sorry, but your father's…been taken ill. Delia was trying to get you and, when she couldn't, asked for me. I'm very sorry,' she finished quietly.

Fraser put the phone down and rubbed his face. He was sitting on the bed and he was pale and drawn-looking.

'Here,' Saffron said gently, and put a glass of neat brandy in his hand. She'd changed back into her shorts and T-shirt while he'd been on the phone.

He looked at it, sniffed it, then downed the tot in one swallow. 'Thanks. By the way, I owe you an apology.'

'Don't worry about it. How is he?'

'Comfortable. I can't believe it.' He closed his eyes briefly. 'We nearly lost him a few years ago, but he pulled through that illness. Now this.'

Saffron hesitated then sat down on the bed beside him. 'He obviously means a lot to you.'

He said, after a while, 'Yes. My mother died when

I was two and Diana was four. He…bore the burden of both of us, including our disinclination to share him with anyone.'

'That's why he didn't remarry?'

'Well—' he grimaced '—one of the reasons, I suspect. And that's why I was rather happy to see him so taken with Delia.'

'I've got the feeling Delia's just as taken. She was distraught. Isn't it strange? They've only just met.'

'Love at first sight,' he said dryly, and looked down at her.

Their gazes clashed then a faint smile twisted his lips. 'You didn't have to change. I would have survived the onslaught of your nightwear despite what I may have intimated to the contrary.' He paused and his dark gaze became intent. 'Did you really imagine I would have gone straight to Cathy?'

'I…' Saffron laced her fingers together and wished a convenient hole would open up at her feet. 'It crossed my mind,' she said. 'Helped along by the fact that you weren't in your room, you see,' she added earnestly, and made the mistake of looking up at him. To see sheer, wicked amusement at her obvious discomfort. 'There's no need to look like that,' she said shortly. 'Anyone would think it's unheard of!'

'Depends what kind of man, or woman, you are, I guess,' he offered gravely.

She considered. 'What do you mean?'

'Put it this way—if the *right* person is not available, then the wrong one is even more out of the question. Is that how it would work for you, do you think?'

'Definitely.'

'Why do you imagine it would be different for me, then?'

Saffron opened her mouth, closed it and sighed deeply.

He waited a moment then reached for the phone.

'What are you doing?' she asked.

'Changing our flight to an earlier one if I can. Any objections?'

'No. Of course not.'

He put the phone down a few minutes later. 'Nine o'clock.'

'Good.'

'So. All that remains to be said once again is—goodnight.'

'Fraser,' she said abruptly. 'Why do you...want me?'

He raised an eyebrow at her. 'Why shouldn't I?'

'I mean—' she paused frustratedly '—I seem to amuse you an awful lot. And I don't often seem to get the opportunity to be other than angry, misunderstood or misunderstanding. Are you sure I'm not just an utter novelty?'

'Saffron,' he said slowly. He made to take her hand then appeared to think better of it. 'I wanted you from the moment I saw you dancing by in your lovely dress. A novelty? When I discovered your extreme disapproval, perhaps. But, if you doubt everything else, don't doubt that.'

His dark gaze roamed her face and her figure. She'd tied her hair back with a green ribbon, he noted, and discovered he would love to undo it. Her white T-shirt had little green dots on it, and the green leather belt of her white shorts emphasised her small waist.

The smooth skin of her arms and legs was faintly perfumed as if she'd recently used a body lotion. Her face was entirely innocent of make-up, and once again he was struck by her unusual looks.

You couldn't call Saffron Shaw conventionally pretty, he mused, because her face was neither conventional nor merely pretty. Her green eyes were striking. The way she held her head beneath that heavy mass of hair was proud and sometimes defiant, her perfect skin was an invitation alone, and as for her mouth... He grimaced inwardly and found himself wondering what kind of fool Simon Harris had been. And wondering if she would ever get over him.

'The same for me.' Saffron stopped as if she hadn't realised she was speaking her thoughts aloud. 'I mean, it *was the same*, I have to admit,' she said then in a suddenly shaken voice as the way he was looking at her brought back memories of being in his arms in her beautiful dress, and how her thoughts had got carried away even then.

'You chose to deny it at the time and for quite some time afterwards,' he reminded her.

'For all sorts of good reasons,' she parried with more spirit. 'I didn't know you from a bar of soap at the time. You could have been...' She shrugged.

'A regular Bluebeard?' he suggested with a touch of amusement. 'Not to mention a pirate.'

'If you think being Fraser A. Ross is any guarantee that you aren't an absolute heel with women, it's not, you know.'

'Quite right,' he agreed. 'Are we straying from the point, though? You didn't know who I was at the time but you must know me much better by now, Saffron. So, what are you trying to say?'

Saffron bent her head and concentrated fiercely on pleating the hem of her shorts.

He watched her working fingers and the slim line of her back with narrowed eyes until she looked up abruptly. He raised an eyebrow at her.

'I still believe it couldn't work for us, but perhaps—' she swallowed '—we need each other just for the time being?'

'How do you think you need me, for the time being, Saffron?' he asked very quietly.

She breathed uncertainly then looked across the room towards the verandah. 'This may sound strange, or crazy, but there's a whole alien island out there—lovely as it is—that makes me nervous, lonely and sad. I—can usually cope with all that when I'm home and busy. Tonight, I don't seem to be coping at all well.'

'Go on,' he said barely audibly.

'Then there's you, concerned and...'

'Frustrated?' he suggested.

She took a breath. 'Are you?'

He smiled but this time unamusedly. 'Oh, yes.' He paused and searched her eyes. 'But, Saffron, things don't always work that way. One-night stands require a degree—'

'I wasn't suggesting a one-night stand!'

'How long, then? For the three weeks you've set aside to do my house?'

Saffron tore her gaze away and discovered she was breathing rapidly and unevenly as well as starting to feel foolish. 'You're right. I can't believe I did that...'

'Look,' he said after a time, 'it's been an emotional evening. Not the best time for making decisions like this. And especially not the best way to try to forget another love.'

She opened her mouth to protest but closed it abruptly. And she smiled shakily as she said with a little gesture, 'Then all that's left to say is goodnight again. You were right!' She stood up and reached for the walking stick.

He didn't. He looked at her instead—at the way her chin was tilted, how she leant lightly on the stick, how green her eyes were and how reserved her expression was. And it stirred him curiously, he discovered, to think of her being afraid of the night and an alien place out there, to see a basic insecurity in someone normally so assured. To see a vulnerable girl beneath the spirit and fire that usually went to make up Saffron Shaw.

He sighed and said, 'On the other hand, there's no reason on earth why we shouldn't do this. We certainly seem to enjoy it.'

'What do you mean?'

'Why, this,' he said gravely, and, standing up at last, took her in his arms.

'Fraser,' she whispered, her eyes stunned, 'what are you doing?'

'Kissing you goodnight, Saffron, that's all.'

'That's all,' she murmured beneath her breath a little later.

She was lying in his arms on the bed although she didn't remember much about how they'd come to be there. She did remember trying to resist him, but not for long, especially when he'd said quietly and as if to a child, 'Don't be silly, Saffron. I'm not going to hurt you.'

Then, as it had before, the magic had started to take over and his hands had moved on her in a way that had made her heartbeat do silly things. And his mouth had worked its own magic, teasing her lips apart, and his body had felt hard and honed against hers, and her soul had thrilled to it all. Her body had felt like a wand in his arms, reed-slim and pliable, softening, aching to be even more intimate.

'Saffron?'

'Mmm?' She moved her cheek against his shoulder now.

'You said something I didn't catch.'

'Did I? Yes, I did. Uh—that didn't seem—I mean, that was rather momentous, you know. Not just a goodnight kiss.' She smiled against his shirt. 'What are you going to do now?'

'Bring you back to earth; bring us both back to earth,' he said ruefully. 'I didn't intend to—go this far.' He pushed himself up on one elbow and smiled down at her, tucked some hair back into her ribbon, traced the outline of her mouth then kissed the tip of her nose. 'Goodnight, sweet Saffron.' He sat up.

She stiffened, and in the moment before she did it had the wit to wish she could stop herself, the wit to wish Delia or *someone* was there to say a cautionary word, but there was no one. And there was, building up in her, a sense of maltreatment, a sense of outrage towards this man who ignited her and was now prepared to walk away from her.

And then there was her own nature, which she often grappled with and mostly managed to contain by channelling the impetuosity and hot-headedness into her work. But just sometimes, she had to admit, she had no control over the things Saffron Shaw said or did...

'Oh, no, you don't, Fraser,' she said grimly, and sat up on her heels, ignoring the pain in her ankle.

He swung round and raised an ironic eyebrow at her. 'Oh, no, I don't what, Saffron?'

'Think you can call all the shots! Think you can kiss me like that then walk away from me. Think you can threaten me, blackmail me and deceive me—'

'If you think it's going to be easy to walk away from you, Saffron, you're wrong,' he said roughly, then paused to add wryly, 'I'd like to know how you think you can stop me.'

That did it. 'Why, like this,' she said sweetly although her eyes were glinting green fire. She pulled her T-shirt over her head and threw it away.

'Saffron...' He set his teeth and a nerve flickered in his jawline.

She raised her hands to her head, released the ribbon and let it float to the bed and ran her hands through her hair to let it settle slowly. Then she put her hands on her hips and followed his gaze, which was resting on her white cotton bra embroidered with red rosebuds. With a shrug, she reached behind her to release it, and it, too, she threw away.

He studied her harshly—the pale, delicate skin of her shoulders just brushed by the shining luxury of her russet hair, the taut, high little breasts, and tiny waist disappearing into her shorts, her slender thighs—and he took her wrists in one hard hand.

'Look, stop it,' he ordered. 'You'll only regret it, you know.'

'No, I won't,' she countered with her head held high. 'And I'll tell you why. I'll have been honest with you and with myself but, more importantly, I won't have been treated as I've been treated *all* the way from the Spences' dinner dance. I'll at least have called *one* of my own shots.'

He released her wrists abruptly. 'And you think that you in this hellcat mood is conducive to making love, Saffron?'

She shrugged again. 'The more of a hellcat I am, the more you seem to like it, Fraser.' And she sat proudly back on her heels, naked to the waist, with her hands on her thighs. 'I'll tell you what else I think. You shouldn't have kissed me the way you did, Fraser Ross.'

'And now I'm going to pay the penalty?' he said softly but lethally. 'By trying to walk away from all this?'

'It's up to you.'

'If I thought you knew exactly what you were doing, Saffron,' he said evenly, 'I—'

'I do. Don't for a moment imagine I make a habit of this. But *I* needed to make a statement.'

There was utter silence for about two minutes. Then he reached out a hand and cupped her breast, and felt the pink, velvety nipple start to unfurl beneath his fingers. He looked down at it for a long moment then into her eyes which were proud and stern. And with a groan he took her into his arms and lay back with her. 'You—I've never met anyone quite like you, Saffron Shaw,' he said into her hair.

'I...' All of a sudden she started to tremble. 'I...s-sometimes *I'm* not quite sure about myself, you know. But there are some things I just have to do so—'

'Hush.' He put a finger against her lips. 'I know. You're also exquisite.'

It was like a slow dance from then on, and it was a revelation to Saffron. She was going to tell Fraser this at one stage then thought better of it.

The private, shadowy place she'd imagined when they'd first met became real as he operated the remote control beside the bed and turned off all the lights, bar one lamp. And he took his shirt off and took her in his arms again. 'We're equal now,' he said gravely.

'Did you...did you really have this fantasy that night, that first night?' she asked with a catch in her voice and an oddly tremulous little smile.

He held her away from him, and the lamplight played over their different skin tones—the pale ivory texture of hers against his darker-toned skin. But it highlighted more—her delicateness against his hard-muscled arms and chest.

'I really did,' he said softly. 'I had this—stranger fantasy even. That you had nothing on at all under your dress.'

Her eyes widened. 'But I did.'

His lips twisted. 'I believe you.' He cupped her breasts and she took a breath. 'It was obviously wishful thinking.'

She put out a hand tentatively and he took it and put it on his chest, covering it with his, and she said with a husky little chuckle, 'There wasn't a lot under that dress, I have to confess.'

'No?'

'No. I wasn't even as well-dressed as I am now, speaking relatively.'

'Very relatively,' he said wryly. 'But we could always remedy that.' He laid her back and undid the belt of her shorts. Once they were off he looked into her eyes and teased, 'Getting closer?'

Her bikini briefs matched her bra—white cotton embroidered with red rosebuds. 'Yes,' she whispered.

He bent over her and kissed her. 'Red roses,' he murmured. 'How appropriate.'

'Why do you say that?' She moved as he started to slide the briefs down.

'A soft and fragrant heart beneath the thorns. A gorgeous, soft and fragrant heart.' The briefs slid off over her ankles, and he stood up to deal with the rest of his clothes.

Saffron turned on her side with her cheek on her hand to watch, and thought he was a joy to behold— her very own pirate. And thought how nice it would be if this were his galleon and she were his captive...

'Why the secret little smile?' he asked, coming back to her.

All her senses stirred as they lay facing each other, their bodies just touching.

'My own private fantasy,' she admitted. 'Am I so prickly, though?'

'Tell me about your own private fantasy.' He slid his hand down her back and cupped her hip. 'And I'll tell you how prickly you are.'

Her lips curved. 'I already have, but I was just thinking about being a captive on board your galleon...'

'A willing captive?'

'Oh, yes. That is to say—'

'Don't.'

'Don't what?'

'Spoil it. You've got me feeling very much a pirate lover right now.' His dark eyes were wicked.

'I love the sound of that. Which just goes to show that I can't be too prickly after all!' She moved closer and slipped her hands around his neck.

'All the best roses have some thorns, Saffron.' He buried his head between her breasts.

'Fraser,' Saffron gasped much later.

All the lights were out this time because there was moonlight streaming into the room, turning the verandah tiles to a sheet of silver and frosting their outlines. He had drawn the pillows up behind him and she was sitting astride him, loving the feel of his hands touching her breasts, slipping beneath her hips, cupping and plucking, smoothing and gripping.

She was also returning the compliment, stroking his chest, twirling her fingers through the dark hairs, feeling, as the moments passed, more and more vibrant, taut yet attuned to the rhythm developing between them. Taut with desire and wonder, because it was the second time they'd made love and, lovely as the first time had been, she had only followed his lead, feeling a little inexpert and wary.

But the way he had seemed to understand and had been incredibly gentle and soothed her to sleep after it had released a song in her heart and, when she'd woken to find him watching her, a rush of desire to respond more fully.

And now the desire was singing through her veins

as he carefully drew her down and she experienced more freedom to move and participate with her body in a way that made him say her name as if it was torn from him, then hold her hard as the final moment came for them both.

Sleep didn't come so easily this time.

She lay quivering in his arms for a long time until, finally, he said again, 'Hush.' And he stroked her hair. 'I might have known.'

Some minutes later, when she'd managed to still her intense reaction to the lovely thing that had happened to her, she asked softly, 'What might you have known?'

'That there would be no half-measures for you, Saffron.' He held her against him.

And again she thought of saying that it had never happened for her quite like this. That her previous experience of love had been pleasant but pale by comparison, had never lifted her to the heights he had. Had often been, in fact, a desire to please at the expense of her own pleasure, never an invitation—such as the one Fraser had extended to her—to be an absolute equal.

I didn't even suspect it could be like this, she thought dazedly. 'Will you stay for a while?' she asked, unable to still the suddenly anxious note in her voice, then hid her face in his shoulder. In case, even in the moonlight, he would see her heart in her eyes. Her real fear of being alone and her…love? But perhaps he knew anyway.

He said quietly, 'Of course. I'm here; I'll be here when you wake up.'

She relaxed and revelled in his closeness, the wonderful feeling of strength and protection his arms around her and his body against her gave. And finally she fell asleep.

She woke again, very early, just as the sun was starting to rise, and he was still there beside her, asleep, peacefully.

She stared her fill. She wanted to touch the dark shadows on his jaw, smooth the hair off his forehead, run her hand over his broad shoulder where the sheet had slipped, snuggle against him, but forced herself to resist. She couldn't resist the sheer feeling of well-being, though, and lay on her back, stretched her arms upwards and pointed her toes.

When she turned back to him after that wonderful, sensuous stretch, it was to find that although he hadn't moved he was watching her lazily.

'Hi,' she said softly. 'Sleep well?'

'Mmm.' He drew the sheet away from her.

'Oh,' Saffron said, and tried to draw it back, unsuccessfully.

His lips twitched. 'I love looking at you, that's all.'

'Well—'

'I've been plagued by wanting to do this for a while now,' he added gravely. 'There was that beautiful, strapless dress to start with. Then a shirt and daisy-splashed leggings. And of course your flying suit had an effect on me that you may remember.' He raised a wry eyebrow at her.

'Yes,' she said sternly, then chuckled.

'All of which,' he continued, 'hid to various degrees...all this.' He sat up suddenly and gazed down at her.

'I…had never thought it was particularly special,' she said on an uneven breath.

He looked into her eyes quizzically. 'What do they say about the best things coming in small parcels? I thought I told you last night that you were exquisite.'

'Really?'

'Yes. Pale, beautifully curved, satiny and perfect. As for these…'

He touched each nipple and watched as they changed beneath his fingers from tight buds to standing erect. Then he bent his head and tasted each one delicately. 'You never told me whether you liked this,' he said with a wicked little glint, looking into her eyes.

'I should have thought it was obvious,' she whispered as a wash of sheer desire rippled down her body and her hands closed rather desperately on his shoulders. 'I…love it.'

'I'm glad,' he replied. 'So do I.'

But his gaze became preoccupied with her body again, as did his hands, sliding slowly down her waist and hips, his fingers dallying in the springy curls that matched her hair, then going on to her thighs.

Saffron cleared her throat but her voice was still unusually husky as she smoothed her hands across his shoulders. 'May *I* say that you leave…other pirates for dead, Mr Ross?'

A silent laugh jolted him then his fingers moved upwards again and this time they did more than dally. Talk about exquisite, Saffron thought dizzily as they wrought the most exquisite sensations upon her with the lightest touch. So much so that her eyes widened beneath his intent gaze, her lips parted, her fingers

dug into his shoulders again and her body shuddered
with sheer pleasure.

'How…why did you do that?' she gasped.

'Did you mind?'

'No. Oh, no, but—'

'Good. I just felt like being a pirate again, I guess.'

She smiled, and an imp of mischief grew in her
eyes. 'What is the feminine name for a pirate?'

His gaze narrowed and he slipped his hands around
her waist. 'I don't think there is one. Why?'

'I just felt like showing you I could be one too.'

'Ah.' He released her and lay back with his hands
above his head in a classic gesture of surrender. 'You
have my full approval.'

Saffron turned over and rested her fists on his chest,
and her chin on her fists. 'I've changed my mind,' she
confided. 'I think I'll leave it so as to surprise
you. I'm sure pirates are particularly effective when
they use the element of—' But she stopped abruptly,
her eyes widening again.

There was a moment's silence, then he sat up and
pulled her up beside him so they were sitting side by
side. He pulled the sheet up across their knees. 'Saffron—'

But the phone rang.

They stared into each other's eyes for a moment,
then he picked it up.

'Not bad news?' she asked fearfully when he put
it down again.

'I'm afraid so; my father's had a bit of a relapse.
Look, Roger—Diana's husband, Roger Marr—has or-
ganised a seat for me on a Lear jet that's landing here
in an hour. It's a private flight, not a commercial one,

and there's only one seat available, but it'll get me home hours before I would have been there otherwise. Saffron—'

'Don't worry about me, Fraser,' she said urgently. 'Can I—help you pack or something?'

His eyes softened as they rested on her upturned face. 'You're a brick. Listen.' He took her in his arms. 'They've moved him to Brisbane so it may be a few days before I—'

'Go and have a shower, Fraser,' she advised gently, and kissed his cheek lightly.

'But I don't want you to—'

'I won't— I'll be fine, believe me. Will you get up and go?'

But leaving Hamilton Island and the beautiful Whitsundays proved to be a sad experience for Saffron.

She spent the last half-hour before the coach was due to come to take her to the airport sunk deep in thought as she watched the diamond-studded water lap the beach below her verandah. Watched the brightly colored sails of little catamarans skim the surface of the sea as a light breeze blew and Passage Peak presided over it all.

And she remembered standing on that same beach in the moonlight, so enthralled by Fraser Ross that she'd tripped carelessly and sprained her ankle. She turned inside at last only to be confronted by the memory of her actions the previous night. Taken, she told herself, against the genuine conviction that this man was not for her...

* * *

'Why, Saffron,' Cathy said, bending over her with a tray as the flight got under way, 'where's Fraser?'

'Left a little earlier, Cathy. Thanks.'

'How was the night?'

Saffron froze with a glass of juice to her lips and eyed the other girl, once again so poised and polished in her uniform. 'What do you mean?'

'I saw you two in the passage last night. An hour or so later I rang Fraser but there was no reply. Could it be that you're more than his interior decorator now?'

Saffron couldn't hide the tide of colour that crept up her throat, but she set her lips resolutely.

'If so,' Cathy went on with a rather dry little smile, 'I wouldn't hold out for a wedding ring. Mistress material maybe, but wife? I suspect that whoever she is she'll be much more—exclusive than you or me.' She moved away smoothly.

Saffron closed her eyes and laid her head back bleakly.

'Delia, this is a surprise,' Saffron said as she walked into the arrivals lounge.

'Fraser rang me and asked me to pick you up,' Delia replied. 'Any luggage to collect?'

'No. I got it all on as hand luggage.' Saffron paused and eyed Delia sharply. 'How is he? His father, I mean.'

'Holding his own; that's all they can say at the moment.'

'Well, shouldn't you be staying up here in Brisbane instead of driving me back to the Gold Coast?'

Delia smiled wanly. 'I'm not that welcome.'

'Fraser?' Saffron queried incredulously.

'No. He was very nice on the phone, but Diana—well, earlier she…' Delia trailed off.

'I can imagine. Bitch.'

Delia started to walk towards the main entrance. 'We don't really know each other that well, Saffron. Bernard and I.' She shrugged and gestured. 'The car's this way. The thing is, I didn't feel it was right to cause—tensions in the family at a time like this.'

Saffron was silent, digesting this. Then she said, 'Fraser approves, by the way. I'm sure that if he feels his father needs you he'll let you know.'

'Thanks. I wondered how he knew—I suppose you told him?'

'I think his father may have intimated something to him too.'

'I still can't believe it happened so quickly, so—' Delia broke off and squared her shoulders. 'How did it go?'

'Go?'

'The job. His house—the reason you went up there.'

'Oh, that.' Saffron winced inwardly but patted her briefcase. 'It went very well. Should be able to get cracking with some orders and so on as soon as I get back to the office.'

'So he was easier to work with than you expected?' Delia unlocked her car with a lurking little smile then frowned suddenly. 'Why are you limping?'

'I fell over and sprained my ankle. It's much better but I could have done with the walking stick for another day or so, only it was a borrowed one—well, I forgot it anyway.' She climbed into Delia's car carefully.

'And he *was* easy to work with?' Delia asked as she switched on the ignition and adjusted the rearview mirror.

'Do you know,' Saffron said slowly, 'I doubt if I'll find anyone easier?' She put her hand to her mouth briefly. 'And I'm very much afraid I did something in the heat of the moment that I might regret for the rest of my life.'

CHAPTER SEVEN

'SAFFRON, I'm worried about you,' Delia said the next morning, as soon as she arrived at work.

'Join the club—I mean, I'm worried about *you*,' Saffron said lightly, but added seriously, 'How are you coping?'

'Feeling better now that I know Bernard came through the operation all right.'

Bernard Ross had had a heart bypass operation the previous afternoon and, although he was still in Intensive Care, the prognosis was good. Saffron had heard this herself through a phone call from Fraser last evening. It had not been a long call and he'd sounded clipped and strained although he'd made a point of asking her how she was. And she'd made a point of assuring him she was fine and telling him he should concentrate on his father.

'Here's the paper,' Delia said, putting it down on the desk. 'He's front-page news. I suppose you've been here since the crack of dawn? How about me getting you some breakfast?'

'That'd be lovely, Delia. I don't know what I'd do without you.'

Saffron picked up the paper as Delia left.

There were two photos on the front page, one of Bernard Ross and one of Fraser. It was the one of Fraser she studied. He was wearing a suit and tie, leaving a building with a rather august portico, and the glance the photographer had captured was cool and unimpressed. In fact the whole picture captured a man who was obviously powerful but hard to pin down, good-looking, intensely assured...and a far cry from the man she'd slept with only two nights ago.

She swallowed suddenly and read the accompanying article. It was a brief report of Bernard's illness then a résumé of the Ross empire, going back to Fraser's great-grandfather who had started it all. It was also a tribute to both Bernard and Fraser Ross but particularly Fraser, for his business acumen, which had seen the empire expand, and, most importantly, continue to flourish when others had expanded and fallen.

There was also a bit about Fraser's early life—an impressive school, a first at Oxford, a rowing blue and a prestigious, world-renowned yachting trophy to his credit.

Saffron's eyes were widening as she read this when Delia arrived back with breakfast.

'A toasted bacon and egg sandwich, a muffin, an apple and coffee. Sound OK?'

'Yes. Thank you. I didn't know he was a yachtsman!'

'Who?'

'Fraser—haven't you read this?' She handed the paper to Delia.

Delia sat down and pulled her own coffee towards her. 'Oh, yes. His father mentioned it. He's given it up although he still has a boat. Didn't you see it? It was moored at the jetty the night we went to dinner.'

Saffron shrugged. 'I wasn't in any mood to be looking out for boats; no, I didn't. Impressive?'

'Well, I'm not an expert but it looked to be a very trim yacht. What was its name?' Delia frowned. 'Oh, I remember—*Buccaneer*— What's wrong?'

Saffron had choked on her first mouthful of toasted sandwich. 'Nothing—uh—something went down the wrong way. So…why did he give it up?' she asked, striving for some composure.

'His father is of the opinion it wasn't a great love of his life although he obviously enjoyed it. But it was more of a challenge. Something to be mastered. Which he did; he's like that, apparently.'

'And once it's mastered he loses interest,' Saffron said slowly.

'He didn't say that. Apparently Fraser still sails but only as a hobby. He doesn't have the time, for one thing. Saffron—'

'Delia, be a honey and don't,' Saffron said gently.

'But after what you told me in the car on the way home from the airport yesterday I—'

'After what you literally prised out of me in the car on the way home from the airport yesterday, don't you mean?'

Delia grimaced. 'If you hadn't mentioned something you'd regret until the day you died, I might have been less concerned! How can you be so sure he's not for you, Saffron?'

Saffron raised an eyebrow. 'I think it's more a case of I'm not for him, Delia. But, be that as it may, I'd rather not…talk about it.'

'Well, what are you going to do? Have you made a mutual decision of some sort?'

Saffron considered. 'I suppose we did.'

'After…it happened?'

'No. But nothing's changed. Delia, we need to get stuck into this. Could you get my film developed? But, Delia, if you need any time off just say the word—promise me?'

'Thanks, pal.'

Saffron finished her breakfast slowly and gave silent thanks that she was home. She looked around her office and breathed deeply. Whatever life held in store for her—and she had a premonition of pain and a parting—she still had this.

She pulled a pad towards her and started to work again. The day flashed by as she did battle with a louvred-blind-maker who preferred to take his own measurements and was only mollified when asked tartly if her measurements had ever been wrong, and would he like to pay his own way up to the Whitsundays if that was the case.

She went through catalogues of china, crystal, silver and linen, thought about pots and pans, and paid a visit to Marina Mirage to inspect the new consignment of Javanese furniture. She got a surprisingly prompt response from her contact in Zanzibar, but flinched slightly at the cost involved and once again wondered why she'd got carried away on the subject of Zanzibari doors.

She also chose some beautiful rugs, and was thankful that the interior of Fraser's house was all wood-panelled so she didn't have to worry about wall colour schemes. Tomorrow, she told herself, she'd visit some of her favourite galleries looking for *objets d'art*.

It was nine o'clock when she got home, feeling

weary and drained. She had a shower, put on her green towelling robe, made some toasted cheese, put Enya's *Watermark* CD on, and sat cross-legged on her sumptuous buttermilk-coloured couch.

The doorbell rang.

She sighed, frowned and hesitated. It rang again.

'I'm coming,' she called, sliding off the couch and tripping on the rug.

Consequently she was breathless and annoyed when she finally wrenched the door open. It was Fraser, in jeans and a navy jumper, with his hair wind-blown. She saw past him to the Mercedes in the drive with the hood down.

'Oh. You!' she gasped.

'Yes,' he agreed. 'Who were you expecting?'

'No one! That's—'

'Then perhaps you should have put some more clothes on,' he murmured with a twisted little grin.

Saffron looked down to see that the edges of her robe had parted company to reveal clear skin down to her pale yellow bikini briefs. 'Damn,' she muttered as she drew them together and tightened the sash. 'I...tripped,' she explained.

'Not again—any damage? May I come in, by the way? Unless you'd prefer to be kissed on the door-step?' His dark glance was entirely wicked.

'Come in,' she said hastily, and led him through to the lounge. 'I wasn't expecting you—Fraser!'

But she got no further. In fact, when she could speak again they were seated on the couch with their arms around each other, her head on his shoulder. Enya was soaring through 'Orinoco Flow', somewhat reflecting Saffron's feeling that she was sailing away into ecstasy.

'How is he?' she murmured, rubbing her cheek against the wool of his jumper.

'He's doing pretty well. It's still a bit early to tell but, if it's successful, they tell me this operation should make a new man of him.'

'I'm so glad.'

'Mmm. I hate hospitals.' He sighed and rubbed his jaw. 'Diana's with him. But I should go back tonight. So.' He looked around. 'This is genuine Saffron Shaw?'

'All my own work,' she answered pertly, and sat up. 'What would you like? Something to eat? Drink? Oh!'

'What?'

'I forgot about my toasted cheese. Never mind; it's not completely cold.' She nibbled at a slice.

'Is that dinner?' he asked quizzically.

'Yep! Like a slice?'

'No, thanks.' He grinned wryly. 'Not only don't I like cold toasted cheese, but I couldn't bear to deprive you of any food. On the other hand, I could do with a drink— Stay there.' He got up. 'Tell me where it is and I'll get it.'

Saffron wrinkled her nose. 'Well, there's a bottle of red wine in the rack in the kitchen—and that's the full extent of it.'

He laughed and ruffled her hair and walked through to the kitchen. When he returned after a few minutes, he brought with him not only the wine and two glasses but also a selection of cheese, salami, pickled onions, olives and gherkins on a board.

'I wondered what you were doing!'

'Raiding your fridge. Do you mind?'

'No, of course not. Only I feel guilty—you haven't eaten, have you? I should be whipping up something only I'm not terribly good at it...'

'Hush, sweet Saffron,' he advised, and poured the wine. 'Tuck in; if I know you, you need it. How's Delia?' He sat back down beside her and stretched his long, jeans-clad legs.

'Worried and—' Saffron bit her lip.

'I was going to suggest that she come up to see my father not tomorrow but the next day. They'll still be doing tests and he'll be hooked up to all sorts of machines, but I know he'd like to see her.'

'Oh!' Saffron's face lit up. 'Could she? She'd be thrilled. But...' Her face fell. 'Diana...?'

'Leave Di to me. Roger's back in residence anyway. That should take her mind off too much mischief. They're having a reconciliation.'

'I see.'

He looked down at her wryly. 'What do you see?'

Saffron hesitated, unsure whether to speak her mind. 'Nothing really.'

'Now, Saffron, I know you well enough to know there must be something,' he teased. 'Spit it out.'

'You may not like it.'

'When has that ever stopped you?' he asked with a trace of irony.

'Well, then, on behalf of the female sex in general—in general, mind—I rather resent the implication that without a man in our lives we're prone to mischief.'

'I wasn't generalising,' he said after a slight pause.

'See?' She glanced up at him.

'I didn't think you liked my sister.'

'I don't. That is, for reasons best known to herself, she didn't seem to like me. As a matter of fact I know exactly why she doesn't like me. She thinks I'd be highly unsuitable wife material for you, Fraser. Would I be wrong in divining that she also thinks you've got to a slightly dangerous age in regard to the state of matrimony?'

'What are you trying to say, Saffron?' he countered impatiently. 'If there's one thing women deserve being lumped into a category over, it's their eternal preoccupation with the state of matrimony.'

The silence was crashing as even Enya clicked off just as he finished speaking. And they stared into each other's eyes, Saffron's darkening, his cool and taunting.

'I don't have that problem in regard to you, Fraser,' she said, speaking precisely and coldly. 'I always knew marriage would be impossible for us. But, just as a matter of interest, what is your problem with it? And as a further matter of interest, although academic now, what did you have in mind for me? Mistress? Part-time lover? Until the right wife came along? Perhaps even *after* she came along?'

'Well, the hellcat didn't stay submerged for long, did it?' he drawled. 'Perhaps you too need to be taken to bed on a very *regular* basis to keep you out of mischief. Oh, no,' he added roughly as her hand flashed out and he caught it inches from his face. 'Keep your fists to yourself, Miss Shaw. Unless you *would* like me to rip your clothes off and make love to you on the floor?'

Saffron panted as she tried to wrest her wrist free, causing him to smile unpleasantly and say sardonically, 'Not that there's an awful lot to rip off.'

She glanced down and closed her eyes in sheer frustration because, with her exertions, her robe had parted again but even more revealingly this time. 'Let me go,' she said urgently.

He did so, but added insult to injury by closing her robe up to her chin for her, tightening the sash and smiling wryly into her eyes. He also said, 'Listen, no one in their right mind would start making wedding lists at this stage so if that's what you're holding against me, Saffron, don't you think you're being a little premature?'

She put her hands to her face and tried desperately to think. She also cursed herself for allowing this to blow up out of nothing. She *didn't* like his sister and thought it quite likely that her sour marriage *was* souring her, but…why shouldn't it? And why should men consider that all the worries of a woman's world could be solved by sex?

'Saffron?'

She took her hands away and breathed deeply. 'Am I being a little premature? No,' she said sadly. 'That's what I tried to explain to you about me. That's what—'

'Before you seduced me?' he interrupted with detached interest.

Saffron bit her lip then clenched her fists. 'Let's not forget who started this,' she said bitterly.

'But I'm interested. Did nothing change *after* you seduced me?'

'Will you stop saying that?' she flashed angrily.

'Why? Isn't it true?' His eyes mocked her.

'Only after you kissed me most— Oh, what the hell?' She slid off the couch and stood in front of him with her hands on her hips. 'Nothing changes the fact that I'm not the right wife for you, and nothing changes the fact that you don't really know what kind of wife you want—only that it's about time you got one!'

He stood up as well and for a moment he was terrifyingly tall, tough and together. 'So on the basis of all this surmise I'm getting my marching orders; is that it, Saffron?'

Her shoulders slumped slightly. 'Fraser, it wouldn't work. I think we both know it wouldn't work,' she said huskily. 'Tell me honestly that I'm wrong…about you.'

The silence lasted for a full minute. 'Well, I *can* tell you one thing,' he said at length. 'We'll never know. Will you finish the house?'

Her lips parted as she stared at him. 'Not if you don't want me to,' she said barely audibly.

'Oh, I do. I don't back out of my business deals, Saffron.'

'But—'

'I didn't think you did either.' His gaze was hard.

'It means we'll have to—' she swallowed '—stay in touch.'

'Perhaps you should have thought of that before you sent me on my way, in a manner of speaking.' This time his gaze was darkly insolent as it raked her from head to toe, and carried an unmistakable meaning which he then chose to make crystal-clear. 'Going to miss me—actually touching you, Saffron?'

She turned away suddenly. 'I think you'd better go.'

'I'm on my way,' he said from right behind her. 'Don't bother to see me out.' But he put his hands on her shoulders and turned her to face him, to add with a shade of malicious amusement, 'Come now—tears? I thought you were tougher than that.'

She straightened her spine although the green of her eyes remained drenched. 'I will be, Fraser. I will be.'

'Good.' He kissed her lightly on the brow. 'Fare thee well, then, my hellcat interior decorator. Until we meet again. I wonder what we'll find to do battle about then. Zanzibari doors?'

And, with this parting shot, he left.

Saffron waited until she heard him drive away then she collapsed onto the couch and burst into serious tears. Why? she asked herself. Why choose tonight to have an argument with him when he came all this way to see you? When he was obviously tired and had had enough of hospitals…? Why?

She wiped her eyes with the back of her hands and lay full-length with her head cradled in the cushions, just lay until the shuddering sobs subsided. Then she sat up and picked up her wineglass, which she hadn't touched, and took a long draught, welcoming the harsh taste of it before the body took over. She stared at the glass miserably.

'Because being right about anything doesn't exactly recommend itself to you at the moment?' she asked herself softly. 'Because you've fallen in love with him? And are horribly afraid he hasn't? What if he said he had—and asked you to marry him? What would you have done then?'

She drank some more wine and closed her eyes as she wondered what made her think that something she couldn't do for another man would be possible for Fraser Ross. Giving up her career in other words.

But I didn't get asked, or told I was loved, she reminded herself. So what was I supposed to do? Tear myself to pieces over a man who may never love just one woman? No, she thought, it's better this way—a far, far better thing...

She grimaced as she reminded herself of Sydney Carton going to the guillotine at the end of *A Tale of Two Cities*. Then she deliberately reminded herself of the anguish she'd suffered over Simon Harris, only, she discovered, Simon seemed to have paled into insignificance suddenly.

She got up abruptly, afraid to delve too deeply into the significance of *that*, and took herself off to bed.

'They're home,' Delia said some days later.

It was a Monday; not that that made much difference to Saffron. She'd worked right through the weekend.

'That's nice. They don't keep them in long, do they?'

Delia shrugged. 'Five or six days. They got home yesterday afternoon. I spent an hour with Bernard. Fraser is spending the rest of the week with him.'

She glanced at Saffron, who said casually, 'Good. What about Diana?'

'She and Roger have gone away for a few days— without their children. Apparently there's a—'

'Reconciliation under way,' Saffron finished for her prosaically, and stuck her pen behind her ear. 'Let's hope it lasts, from your point of view. Delia, do you think cream is a good colour for a man? To be sat upon, as in a lounge suite?'

Delia paused, as if she'd been about to say something else, and asked, 'Why?'

'Well, I like it so much when it's set against a lot of wood but I can't help wondering how practical it is. Look at this.' She showed Delia a photo of a lounge suite, broad and comfortable and covered in cream linen. Then she showed her the sketch she'd made of it in the main lounge of Fraser Ross's house, a sketch now complete with lamps, paintings, tables and chests.

'I think it looks lovely,' Delia said genuinely. 'I adore those two Javanese wooden-backed chairs and that vast, low coffee table. I think the gold screen painted with animals is superb and the Ch'ing marriage cupboard—' she pointed to a tall, red-lacquered, two-door antique cupboard with brass handles '—was *such* a find. But, if you're worried about practicality, why don't you go for cream leather?'

'No,' Saffron said immediately. 'I hate leather except in dens or fuddy-duddy old men's clubs, and I don't think it suits the mood of this room at all, which is supposed to be slightly oriental and mysterious.'

Delia, used to Saffron's decided opinions, remained serene. 'Well, there are other rooms for him to relax in if he's all muddy and fishy or whatever,' she said with a humorous glint. 'But it is supposed to be a masculine setting, I presume—you know what it needs? A tiger skin or a zebra skin draped some-where. Or a stag's head on a wall.'

Saffron raised her eyes heavenwards. 'Don't even suggest it. I'm in enough trouble over Zanzibari doors. Besides, tigers are an endangered species,' she said severely.

'Maybe, but I've never heard that zebras are.'

'That's how they become endangered,' Saffron re-marked. 'Anyway, do they have zebras in Java? I doubt it.'

'And do they have elephants in Zanzibar?' Delia asked sweetly.

Saffron glared at her then burst out laughing. 'Sorry. You know, you're right, though. I need a more masculine influence somewhere, and this plain cream suite simply doesn't supply it.' She tore up the photo and tossed the pieces into the bin under her desk.

'Why don't you ask him what he'd like?' Delia suggested after a moment.

'I tried that,' Saffron said bleakly. 'Whatever else Fraser Ross is, he's not a fountain of ideas to do with decorating.' She started to doodle on a pad.

Delia watched her bent head and felt her heart go out to her boss. Because she had no doubt that things had not been resolved happily between Saffron and Fraser Ross. But how to help? 'A man's man,' she commented quietly, and added suddenly, 'His father is of the opinion that too many women have made fools of themselves over him.'

Saffron's head came up at that and she stared at Delia. 'Do you think I don't know that?' she asked very quietly. 'Do you think I haven't seen it with my own eyes?'

'Have you?' Delia blinked.

'Yes…'

Delia sat back and sighed. 'No one could accuse you of that, Saffron.'

A strangely haunted little smile played on Saffron's lips. In the explanation Delia had wormed out of her on the way back from the airport, she hadn't given any details of just how they'd come to sleep together… 'No,' she said tiredly, however. 'I guess they couldn't. Uh…OK! Lounge suites; I'm on the trail once more!'

'What about—' Delia frowned again '—that lounge suite with *printed fabric* zebra-skin cushions. Scatter cushions, I mean. But not dozens of little fiddly ones. Say, just two large ones in each corner of the couch trimmed with gold braid? He obviously doesn't object to an international flavour otherwise he wouldn't have let you have your head over Java, not to mention Zanzibar. And he obviously doesn't mind a jungle flavour, in theory, if he's OK'd the elephants on the screen.'

Saffron blinked and studied her sketch intently while Delia waited composedly for her idea to be demolished. But her boss surprised her. She got up, came round the desk and kissed her tenderly on the forehead. 'Delia,' she said in her husky voice, 'you're a genius. That's *it*! It's just the touch I need.'

But Delia suddenly looked worried. 'What if he *doesn't* like zebra skin?'

'Then he's stuck with a plain cream linen suite,' Saffron said hardily. 'Delia, I really don't think he cares one way or the other, but I can just see this room on the pages of the *House and Garden Yearbook* now!'

'I still think you ought to consult him.' Delia looked stubborn.

'Over two cushions? He can throw them away if he doesn't like them, once the spread is done. Anyway, he and I are not communicating at the moment in case you hadn't noticed.' Saffron looked at her dryly.

'I'm afraid that's about to end.'

Saffron went still and looked at her assistant narrowly. 'What do you mean?'

'He'd like to see you tomorrow morning. At his father's house. He said to bring the quotes for the Zanzibari doors and the Arab chest. He said—' Delia sighed and shrugged '—that there are a few final things you need to hammer out, such as how to get all the stuff up there, and that by next week he'll be too busy.'

'And did he issue any more edicts?' Saffron enquired with dangerous restraint.

'Ten o'clock tomorrow morning.'

'Hello? I'd like to leave a message for Mr Ross, Mr Fraser A. Ross, please,' Saffron said into the phone some minutes later. Delia had left to deal with someone who had come into the showroom.

'Go ahead,' a brisk though elderly voice replied, leaving Saffron in no doubt that it was Flora MacTavish.

'Uh—it's Saffron Shaw here; is that you, Miss MacTavish?'

'None other, Saffron, none other. How are you?'

'I'm fine, thanks. How are you?'

'Considering I'm seventy-six and have an invalid in the house, considering that Diana has chosen this of all times to go back to her no-good husband, I'm doing remarkably well. What is it you wish me to pass on to Fraser?'

Saffron winced. 'He sent me a message to meet him tomorrow, there at the house, at ten o'clock. I'm afraid I'm unable to make it, but he knows where to find me so he—'

'Young lady,' Flora said sternly. 'I like you, and admire your career et cetera, et cetera. But Fraser is responsible for a vast empire and the well-being of many, many people so he doesn't have the time to be running after little interior decorators, however brilliant they are. You be here tomorrow, Saffron, if you know what's good for you, and don't be late!' The phone went dead.

Saffron took the phone from her ear and stared at it. Then she replaced it carefully, and, dropping her face into her hands, had to laugh.

She wasn't laughing the next morning when she dressed for work.

It was a wet day with the rain lashed by a buffeting south-easterly wind, and consequently cooler than the norm for the time of year.

'Go casual? Go dressy? Don't go at all?' she said to herself as she dismally surveyed her wardrobe. 'It's going to be an impossible—interview. How do you conduct yourself with a man you've slept with so recently then fallen out with so—badly?'

Stick strictly to business, she admonished herself,

and laid her hands on an outfit that was, if nothing else, businesslike.

'*Very* nice,' Delia said approvingly as she took in the taupe suede skirt—short but not too short—and the matching short-sleeved buttoned and belted jacket.

With it, Saffron wore the palest fawn sheer tights and a pair of Chanel patent court shoes, which were two-toned—taupe with black toes and heels. She had a smart black patent purse and a shiny black raincoat over her arm which she dumped over the back of a chair. Her hair was plaited and tied with a narrow black ribbon.

She wore more make-up than normal, Delia noticed, although it was expertly done—and done she suspected, to hide the faint blue circles beneath her boss's eyes that were so often there these days.

'Thanks, Delia,' Saffron said briefly, then smiled faintly. 'I gather you approve of this more than my flying suit?'

'Yes, I do. You look not only lovely but very executive-like. As befitting the owner of that highly successful interior design firm, The Crocus Shop!'

'If you're trying to bolster me up a bit, Delia, you're doing a fine job. Thanks, pal!' She hugged Delia lightly and sat down behind her desk. 'In the meantime—'

'I know—let's get to work!'

CHAPTER EIGHT

FLORA MACTAVISH also approved, apparently as she let Saffron in and took her raincoat.

'So you *can* look like a lady, Saffron,' she said.

'I thought you didn't mind me when I didn't,' Saffron couldn't resist saying with an impish little grin.

'There's a time and place for all things; now's the time for business, I gather. He's in the study; I'll take you down.' And she proceeded to do so. 'By the way, afterwards his father would like to say hello—Mr Ross, Miss Shaw,' she added grandly after a brief tap at the study door.

'Come in, Saffron,' Fraser's disembodied voice said.

She took a deep breath and walked through the door. Flora closed it behind her.

He was on the phone, swivelled round behind the desk to look out over the drenched courtyard, but he swung back and gestured her to a chair opposite him. He didn't interrupt his conversation.

Beyond a bare glance, Saffron did as she was told and started to unpack a pad, pens, a calculator and some notes from her briefcase. She set it all out before her in an orderly fashion then clasped her hands in her lap and waited with her head bent.

'Fine. I'd like it all on my desk by next Monday—

yes, I'll be back in Brisbane by then. Cheers.' Fraser put the phone down and said, 'Well, Saffron?'

She restrained herself from saying, Well, what, Fraser? and confined herself to another brief glance— or tried to. But their gazes clashed and she found she couldn't look away. He was casually dressed in jeans and football jersey, making him look younger but big and dangerous.

She tore her gaze away at last and said tersely, 'Let's just stick to business, Mr Ross.'

'So we're back to that, Saffron,' he murmured. 'Have I suggested otherwise? By the way, you look very...grown-up.' He eyed the lovely soft and supple suede suit, her neat hair with a few raindrops netted in it, her make-up and the tiny pearls in her ears.

'That's precisely what I meant—' She broke off, calmed herself down with an effort and put a folder in front of him. 'Would you go through that, please? It's a list of all the furniture, ornaments, appliances and household goods, et cetera I've deemed necessary for your house, plus their prices. They're all on order but can be changed or cancelled now. Once they're paid for it will be too late.'

He raised an eyebrow but started to read. Then he closed the file, passed it back to her and said, 'Down to the last teaspoon. That's fine, Saffron.'

'Good. I've also taken the liberty of investigating ways and means of getting the whole caboodle up there, and it seems to me the simplest way is to use a carrier. I have a very reliable firm I use a lot. I could arrange for it all to be delivered to their warehouse. They could then pack it into a container and ship it by road to—Airlie Beach?' She glanced at him enquiringly.

'Shute Harbour.'

'OK, Shute Harbour—' she made a note on her pad '—where it can be picked up by barge. If you let me know the name of the barge company you use...?'

He told her and she wrote that down. 'Any questions?' she asked briskly.

He smiled faintly and lay back in his chair at the same time as he twirled a pen in his long fingers. 'It's all very businesslike and impressive, Saffron. Uh, just one—what's the name of the carrier you use?'

She told him, adding that although they were expensive they had a fine reputation for delivering goods intact and on time.

'I'm glad to hear that. They're part of the Ross Group as it happens.'

'Oh!' She looked at him with the first spark of genuine interest in her eyes. 'Oh, good, that'll save a bit of money for you, won't it?'

'Are you interested in saving me money, Saffron?'

'Of course,' she replied severely. 'Good taste may sometimes come at a high price—although not always, believe me—but I am *always* on the lookout for ways to save my clients money. It's only good business sense, I would have thought. For example, you're getting nearly everything there—' she gestured to the folder '—at reduced rates.'

'Do you go out and haggle with your suppliers?' he enquired.

'Why not?'

'Why not, indeed?' But the thought of it obviously amused him. Then he sat forward and flipped open the folder again. 'I didn't see any mention of Zanzibari doors.'

Saffron drew a deep breath, and their eyes locked. 'I decided against them.'

'Why?'

'I thought they were excessively expensive.'

'But they could be got?'

'Yes,' she said rashly. 'I mean—'

'Then why don't you let me be the judge?'

There was a moment's silence as they indulged in a non-verbal clash of wills, a deadly little duel fought by eye contact—Saffron's a brilliant, angry green, Fraser's mocking and dark.

'Very well.' She shrugged as if to say it meant nothing one way or the other to her, and she delved into her briefcase to produce a fax. 'There you are.'

'For a pair of doors no one else in Australia has, for a pair of doors that can even repel elephants or the equivalent, and considering how far they have to come, that's not excessively expensive, Saffron,' he said after a time.

'It would also take three months to get them made and delivered.'

'Is that a problem? It's not as if I'm going to be without front doors for three months.'

Saffron drummed her fingers on the table and chewed her lip, and he watched her dryly.

Then, when she couldn't seem to find anything with which to refute this, he said, 'I bumped into Simon Harris the other day.'

Her lips parted and her eyes widened. *'Where?'*

'Where one generally bumps into doctors—in a

hospital,' he said with considerable irony. 'Did you think I'd sought him out?'

'No. Well, no. But why are you telling me this?'

'Why shouldn't I?'

'But…you spoke to him about me?' Saffron asked dangerously.

'Not precisely, although we did talk about you in the context of both knowing you.' He shrugged.

'I just hope it wasn't in the context of both of you being ex-lovers,' she said in a suddenly suffocated voice. 'How could you?'

'Acquit me,' he answered with a tinge of rough impatience. 'He was the one who brought the subject up.'

'Why?' Saffron blinked confusedly.

'He was part of the team that operated on Dad. Somehow or other after the op, during the course of a conversation along the lines of him recommending that Dad get away for a holiday, the subject of the Whitsunday house came up, and your involvement with it. Strange how life's full of these little coincidences, isn't it?' He looked at her sardonically.

Saffron subsided. 'So what did he say?' As soon as the words left her lips, she could have killed herself, but, of course, it was too late.

And the little look he sent her spoke volumes. 'He was interested to hear how you were getting along,' he drawled. 'He also said that you'd been a memorable acquaintance—something I had to agree with—but I doubt whether he realised the significance of us both having such memorable—memories of you, Saffron. By the way, he's still unattached, if that's of any interest to you.'

'It's not—'

'And still, I would imagine, wondering whether he did the right thing,' he cut across her.

'Wh-what makes you say that?' she stammered.

Fraser shrugged and watched her narrowly for a moment. 'Why would he have gone out of his way to bring you up otherwise? Why would he have looked as embarrassed and troubled as he did? But, you know, I still think you made the right decision *that* time.' He stretched, clasped his hands behind his head and studied her reaction with a dry little smile in his eyes.

If only you knew, Saffron caught herself thinking, and felt herself colour. She dropped her gaze, clasped her hands rather urgently and swallowed. 'I'm sure you're going to tell me why,' she managed to say ironically then.

He laughed softly and sat forward. 'Would you really like me to? I don't think he could have understood you in the slightest, for one thing. I don't believe he really set you alight, for another. Did you ever seduce *him*, Saffron?'

She blushed brightly this time, at the same time as she discovered she would like to kill Fraser Ross. 'And you think you really did set me alight, Fraser?' she said tautly. 'Why, I wonder, if that's the case, did I walk away from *you*?'

'Because you fell in love with me and were afraid I hadn't completely lost my head over you, Saffron?' he suggested with a lethal little smile.

She gasped.

'Hit the nail on the head, I see,' he said gently. 'As for setting you alight—were I to employ my pirate tactics just to see, for example, whether you have little rosebuds embroidered on your bra today beneath your suit of suede armour— Well, we both know how those encounters can get out of hand for us.'

'You…you…' She couldn't go on.

'For that matter,' he drawled, 'were I to kiss you *first*, it might require no pirate tendencies at all; you'd probably do the honours yourself.'

Saffron slammed her chair back and stood up. 'Go to hell, Fraser Ross. And take your blasted house with you.' She picked up the file and flung it at him. 'I'm resigning right here and now!'

But he uncoiled himself from his chair and came round the desk like a dark panther. 'Oh, no, you don't, Saffron.' He took hold of her and sat her down again and kept his hand on her shoulder. 'You'll finish this house otherwise word *will* get spread that The Crocus Shop is unreliable to say the least.'

'You know…' Saffron stopped because her voice was shaking; she was shaking with a mixture of anger and fright. But her combative nature got the better of her. 'You know what's talking, don't you, Fraser? Your fragile ego.'

The hand on her shoulder tightened its grasp briefly then it was withdrawn abruptly and he walked round the desk to sit down and study her expressionlessly. To study the mixture of outrage, injured dignity and bravado in her expression, but also the way she was trying to hide the fact that her hands weren't quite steady.

He set his teeth and wondered briefly if he was going mad. 'All right. Let's get back to business.'

Saffron opened her mouth to say something along

the lines of, That's what I've been trying to stick to all along, but, at a sudden, searing dark glance, changed her mind.

'Very wise,' he murmured, and shuffled papers together savagely. 'I didn't see a quote here for your services, incidentally.'

'Ah. I haven't got around to working that out yet,' she replied after a moment, and somewhat evasively.

He frowned. 'Let's work it out now. I see you have your trusty calculator with you.'

'Um—'

'Saffron,' he warned.

'All right,' she muttered, thought for a bit, then wrote something down and passed the pad to him.

His eyebrows shot up. 'This is ridiculous! For three weeks' work, including weekends, all day and most of the night if I know you, not to mention your inspiration et cetera.'

'It's been a bit of a rushed job so I didn't like to charge you too much.' She swallowed a little nervously at the way his hard eyes played over her, then tilted her chin proudly. 'Besides which, I'm perfectly entitled to charge as little or as much as I see fit.'

'As a statement—another one?' he asked eventually. 'A statement of how little this has all meant to you, Saffron?'

She stared at him and thought, No. A statement to the effect that it's not your fault you didn't fall in love with me, and to the effect that I'll never forget…some things, but…

She looked away suddenly and said stubbornly, 'That's all I'm charging. If the house does get into a magazine, it'll bring me a lot of publicity.' She picked up her briefcase and started to pack it. 'If I could have your cheque, though, for the furniture and goods, I can get all the stuff up there by the end of next week.'

'And?'

'What do you mean?'

'Who supervises the placement of everything up there?'

'Delia will do that. I'm afraid you'll have to pay her fare, but she's very good; she always follows my sketches and instructions to the letter. Of course you'll have to provide some strong men to give her a hand.' She stood up.

He, on the other hand, lay back. 'So you don't intend to see the finished product?'

'I—well, usually I would,' incurable honesty made Saffron say. 'But in this case— Look, I trust Delia.'

'But not me. Or perhaps it's yourself you don't trust?'

Saffron took a breath and ignored the jibe. 'You'll also need a carpenter to install the blinds.'

'Is this goodbye, then, Saffron?'

Help me through these last moments, she prayed to a higher being. 'Yes, Fraser. I'll just go,' she added, and slipped out of the study, closing the door quietly behind her.

Fraser stared at the door then swung round to watch the teeming view from the window at the same time as he was thinking, It wouldn't work; she's right. A hellcat of a little girl when she's not...

He flexed his shoulders as memories of Saffron Shaw in bed came to him. Memories of that curious mix of fire and spirit and uncertainty. A flowering that had taken his breath away, followed by a kind of vulnerability that he couldn't forget.

All the same, he mused with some irony, how would she cope with not being able to do precisely her own thing? For that matter how would I cope? What *did* I have in mind for any wife I took? he asked himself cynically. Certainly not having to adapt my lifestyle to hers... No, we'd drive each other mad. So why am I still doing this? he asked himself grimly.

'Fraser?' Flora stuck her head round the door. 'Fraser, there's been an accident. Saffron—'

He swung round violently and got up precipitately. 'Saffron *what*?'

'She's fine,' Flora said soothingly. 'It happened like this. She was backing out of the driveway in this pouring rain just as your car was being driven in. Your driver claims that, although he saw her and stopped, she didn't see him and just kept coming. But they are both completely unharmed.'

'So?'

'Your car is somewhat smashed, in a very minor way.'

'My Mercedes,' he said slowly.

'Uh-huh. Her car seems to have escaped damage, probably because it has a high-set tow-bar on the rear bumper.'

'She...ran her tow-bar into my car?'

'The near-side door, but only by accident,' Flora assured him. 'She's also covered by insurance, she said to tell you, which will take care of everything. She promised that her insurance company will be in touch immediately.'

'Where is she, Flora?'

'She left. She was terribly embarrassed. I'm surprised you didn't hear anything, but I suppose the rain helped.'

'Get her on the phone for me, Flora.'

Flora drew herself up. 'You wouldn't have chastising the poor child in mind, now, would you, Fraser?'

'Probably. But I also want to make sure she *is* all right,' he answered dryly.

'It's only a car, I know, and I know how much they cost, and that it was custom-made for you, Fraser, or something, but it *is* only a car.'

'Flora,' Fraser said between his teeth, 'if you must know, *you* got me into this whole bloody mess in the first place! Will you get her on the phone?'

'I? Got you into what?'

'Oh, never mind. I'll do it myself.' He glanced around with savage impatience.

'Here.' Flora handed him the phone book regally. 'I must say you're behaving very oddly these days, Fraser. One has to wonder if Diana isn't right.' With this parting shot, she departed stiffly.

Fraser sat down and took a very deep breath.

'Where on earth have you been, Saffron?'

'Delia!' Saffron jumped. It was eight o'clock at night and she'd just let herself into The Crocus Shop. 'What are you doing here?'

'Worried to death about you,' Delia replied bitterly.

'Why?'

'In case you're suffering from delayed shock, whiplash, a bump on the head, or whatever else people who have been involved in a collision can suffer from!'

Saffron took off her raincoat and licked her lips. 'How do you know what happened?'

'Fraser has rung at least three times, and Flora twice more.'

'But Flora knows I was fine,' Saffron objected.

Delia breathed heavily then took in her boss's look of tension and strain, and decided to change tack. 'How did it happen?'

'It was pouring.' Saffron sat down behind her desk and slumped wearily in the chair.

'He had his lights on, apparently—Fraser's driver.'

'I know. I mustn't have been concentrating.' Saffron paused and bit her lip. 'Is he very angry?'

'He's concerned. That you're OK. He didn't sound angry at all.'

Saffron grimaced. 'I wouldn't blame him if he was. I can't believe I did it.' Or believe, she added to herself, that I should have been fool enough to be *crying* at the time, which is really why I didn't see the other car.

'So where were you?' Delia asked.

'I went up to see my brother.'

'All the way to Amberley in this weather?'

Saffron shrugged. 'I needed to have a bit of a break. He's fine. Guess what? He's about to be engaged. To a girl in the RAAF.'

Oh, my dear, Delia thought. You poor kid. 'Ring Fraser,' she suggested. 'After what you did to his car, it's the least you can do.'

'Would you...?'

'No, Saffron,' Delia said firmly. 'Do as you're told!'

Fraser wasn't in as it transpired, but Flora said she would pass on the message. Saffron put the phone down and looked rather helplessly at Delia.

Who said, not without some frustration, 'Home, some supper and bed for you now, Saffron Shaw. Don't argue.'

The next morning, which was the first of the month, saw Saffron changing the window display in her showroom.

She'd pulled down the blind so as not to be visible in her exertions from the pavement, and the new scenario was taking shape. It was a hallway she'd decided to feature this month, with a lacquered French hall table bearing an antique telephone beneath a lovely old Venetian mirror. There was also a pewter bowl of rusty pink and deep blue hydrangeas, white roses and white lilac on the table.

But the highlight of the display was a *trompe-l'oeil* screen she'd found, featuring a hat stand. It was a wooden stand against a saffron background and it bore, like luscious fruit, straw hats trailing ribbons, raffia hats adorned with flowers, a black bowler hat, a little girl's lacy bonnet, a tartan beret—even an army pith helmet with a brass spike.

At the base of the stand there were shoes and boots, polished riding boots, a tiny pair of wellingtons, a frivolous pair of high-heeled sandals and a very oriental pair of slippers with up-turned toes.

She was just standing back to admire the effect when the door opened and Fraser walked in. She dropped the book she had in her hands—a heavy volume of art that she'd been going to put on the hall table—on her toe, yelped, and they both bent to retrieve it at the same time.

'One would almost imagine you were accident-prone, Saffron,' Fraser said, wresting the tome from her oddly nerveless fingers and placing it firmly out of her reach.

She straightened slowly and smoothed the green blouse she wore over her daisy-patterned leggings unnecessarily—an outfit he'd seen her in once before even down to her paint-splashed sand-shoes. Her hair was tied back in a bunch.

He was dressed conservatively in a dark suit, white shirt and a blue and grey polka-dot tie.

'I'm...I'm terribly sorry about your car,' she said miserably. 'I'm sure you must be wondering whether I did it on purpose after what I said, but I didn't. It was...it was the rain, you see. Not only was it very heavy, it was also very noisy.'

He said nothing for a while, just studied her narrowly. Then, abruptly he said, 'Forget about the car. Are you sure you're all right?'

'I'm fine. Honestly!'

'You don't look it.'

Saffron blinked. 'In what way?'

'You look thoroughly washed out if you really want to know—can we go somewhere more private?'

'Thank you!' Saffron said with a toss of her bunched hair and an old-fashioned look. 'Well, I have finished here so, yes, we could go into my office, although, surely it's all been finalised?'

'That's better.' An unamused smile played across

his lips. 'You had me worried for a moment. But there is still this.' He withdrew a cheque from his inner jacket pocket.

'Ah. Yes, please, do come in; I'll write you out a receipt.' She led the way.

'By the way,' she said as she got a receipt book out of her drawer, 'this will go into a trust account. And every penny I spend of it will be itemised and documented with receipts from the suppliers so you'll know I haven't been misusing your money.'

'Very businesslike, Miss Shaw,' he commented.

This time it was a fighting little glance she tossed him. 'I thought we were agreed on that if nothing else.'

He chose not to comment this time, but simply put the cheque down in front of her.

She glanced at it, rustled through the receipt book seeking the right page then stopped dead. 'This—' she picked up the cheque and stared at it '—is *not* what we agreed upon.'

'We didn't agree upon anything, Saffron. You made a—chivalrous—gesture in the matter of your fee, or was it foolhardy? Never mind; I decided not to accept it. It's that simple.' He looked at her impatiently.

'But...'

'No buts, my dear. I got Flora to do some research for me and she is of the opinion that that is what other interior decorators would have charged me, give or take a bit, so that's what you're taking.'

'I...' Saffron bit her lip.

'If you're going to ask me why, I don't choose to

be beholden to you, Saffron,' he said softly but with a curiously cutting little look.

'And you think this will wipe the slate clean?' Why she said it she couldn't begin to imagine, but the words just sprang to her lips.

'Don't you?'

She dropped the cheque and rubbed her face.

He waited, and it was as if the air were charged with static electricity.

It occurred to Saffron as she tried to marshal her thoughts and defences that there was an unspoken challenge in the air, too, but she couldn't pin it down. All she knew, she decided, was that she'd been right when she'd said once—it seemed like a very long time ago—that it would be a bit of a heartache to love Fraser Ross.

This cold, cutting version of him was indisputable proof of that and the sooner she got it all over and done with surely the hurt would begin to recede?

She swallowed and picked up a pen. A minute later, she tore the receipt out neatly along the perforated line and handed it to him. 'Thank you very much,' she said formally. 'I do consider the slate now wiped.' She stood up. 'I'm also sure you're a very busy man so let's not prolong things unnecessarily.'

'There's just one thing that neither of us may be able to wipe, Saffron,' he said after a long moment.

'What's that?' She looked at him wearily.

'An unplanned pregnancy.'

The words were quiet but they seemed to rebound off the walls. Her heart started to beat heavily, and for a moment it seemed to her as if there were only the two of them in the whole world. It seemed as if those dark eyes of his were boring through to her soul and she was flooded suddenly with exquisite memories of their lovemaking.

Besieged by memories of a different Fraser, memories of them naked in the moonlight, when her slightness against the beautiful proportions of his body, her softness against his strength, had been a revelation and a joy...

'No,' she said barely audibly. 'I...if you really want to know why I bumped into your car yesterday, apart from the rain, I...it...well, I tend to be a bit dithery at this time of the month.'

'So.' He stood up as well. 'Then there's nothing more to say?'

She opened her mouth, for a moment unbearably tempted. But she closed it and shook her head.

'Oh, by the way, don't worry about the Zanzibari doors. I've changed my mind.'

She swallowed. 'If you did really want them I could—'

'As a particular reminder of you? I don't think so. You were the one who was anxious not to prolong things unnecessarily, anyway. I think you were right. We'll make this a last, clean cut in other words.' He smiled dryly.

'Why not?' she said very quietly.

'Then goodbye, Saffron. May your business—prosper.'

'And yours, Fraser.' She turned away. She heard him leave.

It was raining again as she lay on her couch that evening, listening to Mozart. Driving rain that slanted against the windows and drummed on the ground.

She'd changed into pyjamas and her green robe, eaten a meal—and couldn't remember when she'd felt more tired, lonely and desolate. *Had* he known? she wondered, reliving once again that piercing moment when the rest of the world had been cut off...at the thought of his child.

The strange part about it was that it had only occurred to her after they'd parted in this very room the night he'd driven down from Brisbane. It had crept into her mind like a seedling breaking the surface of hard ground then clung with an amazing tenacity.

Why? she'd asked herself torturedly. Why would you want the child of a man who doesn't love you? You of all people. This is against all expectations, Saffron, she'd told herself. You're not really—hoping? You couldn't be!

But the plain fact of it had been that she couldn't get the idea out of her mind, and the reason why she couldn't had shaken her to the core. That was how special their lovemaking had been to her. That was how special Fraser Ross would always be to her.

She could hate the fact that he might be cynical and disenchanted, she could query and rail against her own often disastrous impulses and nature that would make her the most unsuitable wife for him, but she couldn't hate the man.

She brushed away a stray tear with her sleeve because of course that little, incredible hope had been no more than that—just wishful thinking. But it was the knowledge of how unexpectedly and deeply it had affected her that had held her silent this morning.

When she had been on the verge of offering to be his mistress—anything to turn the hard, cold man in front of her back to her memories of him, and them.

What was he doing now? she wondered sadly, pillowing her head on her arms. What would he do in the future? Marry a suitable wife, a pliable wife, a wife who would enjoy great privilege—so long as she had no career of her own and was content to fit into his life as he saw fit? A wife who would never make the mistake of trying to get too close? Certainly not a girl who was sometimes a hellcat, who spoke her mind but adored going to bed with him...

He couldn't have doubted that, surely?

A girl who—she swallowed and brushed her eyes again—had been mesmerised at the thought of *their* child. Who couldn't bear to think of him with someone else.

She stared up at the dim ceiling, trying desperately to clear her mind of not only that torment but all her memories of him. All her curiosity about a child of theirs, all her heartbreak. Sleep, creeping up on her at last, was her only release. And she slept the night right through on the couch.

CHAPTER NINE

'WHY on earth do they need them all to be different?' Saffron said savagely, about ten days later.

She'd started work on the guest house project and was contemplating the task of twenty-five bedrooms, all different. 'Don't they realise that even four or five schemes would save them a packet?' she continued to Delia.

'I get the impression it's to be a very classy and different kind of establishment,' Delia murmured.

'I know, stuffed to the brim with antiques, or look-alike antiques,' Saffron muttered darkly. 'Oh, well.' She shrugged. 'It takes all kinds.'

Delia frowned at her bent head. Because normally a project like this would have been an intoxicating challenge for Saffron.

'Why are you looking at me like that?'

Delia started and realised her boss had caught the frown. 'I'm still worried about you,' she admitted.

Saffron grimaced. 'You're very sweet, Delia, but I'll be fine. How's Bernard?'

Delia blushed.

'Like that, eh?' Saffron looked at her impishly then relented. 'I'm *very* happy for you. Does this mean I'm about to lose you, though?'

'Oh, no. We're not going to rush into anything. I'm not, anyway.'

'So he would like to rush you to the altar?' Saffron asked curiously.

'We haven't even got to the stage of going to bed, but, Saffron, I wanted to ask you something.' Delia paused and took a deep breath. 'You know how we had to postpone sending everything up to Fraser's house for a couple of weeks because of the barge being out of action?'

'Uh-huh.'

'Well, Bernard suggested, with Fraser's approval, that we delay it a little longer so...so we could go up together. He and I.'

Saffron sat back. 'Why not? It sounds lovely. Why don't you take a week?'

'I'm not due for holidays yet,' Delia said uncomfortably.

'Who cares? I don't. Look, do it,' she said warmly. 'I've got weeks of creative work here before we get down to the mad rush of actually assembling it all. I can cope!'

Delia sighed and said with difficulty, 'You're... Thanks so much.'

Two days later, at Delia's suggestion, they closed the shop up and treated themselves to lunch in the village.

'I must say you have some good ideas,' Saffron murmured contentedly as they sat opposite the waterfront and watched the world go by. She drew her gaze to Delia. 'But you're not still worried about me, are you?'

'What makes you say that?'

'You almost twisted my arm to get me here, nice

as it's been. I wondered if you were trying to fatten me up, though.'

'I doubt that's possible,' Delia said wryly.

'Take my mind off certain things, then?' Saffron suggested after a moment, and wondered whether it was her imagination that made her think Delia looked suddenly uncomfortable.

'Maybe. You know what we need now? A bit of a walk. Let's go down the jetty.' She stood up.

Saffron grimaced. 'You're full of inspiration and energy, Delia. But I don't—'

'Yes, you do,' Delia said firmly.

'I'm not an invalid, you know,' Saffron said some minutes later as they wandered down between the boats. 'I mean, I appreciate your concern—' She stopped suddenly and narrowed her eyes. They were opposite a sleek yacht, white with a maroon trim, and its name was painted on the bows—*Buccaneer*. 'Isn't this...?'

She turned but Delia had disappeared. She frowned then shrugged, assuming that another boat had caught Delia's attention and that she'd wandered along one of the fingers out of sight to get a better look at it. She turned back.

Was this Fraser's *Buccaneer*? she wondered. And, if so, what was it doing here on the public jetty and not tied up at the house? A little niggle of curiosity possessed her although she tried to fight it. Then she put a hand on the shining timbers of the bow, and walked down the finger alongside it.

'Hello, Saffron,' a quiet voice said above her, and the jetty sank a little as someone leapt lightly down onto its planks—Fraser.

She simply stared at him for a long moment, wondering if she was dreaming. But there seemed no doubt it was Fraser, casually dressed in a yellow T-shirt and khaki shorts with his dark hair wind-blown. Fraser, taking in her slim lime-green capri pants and matching silk shirt, the double gold-link belt around her waist, her loose hair.

'What——?' Her voice didn't seem to want to work. 'What are you doing here?'

'Come to take you away, Saffron.'

Her eyes widened incredulously. 'You can't be serious...'

'Try me.'

'No, look——'

But he picked her up and carried her aboard with no further ado, and sat her in the cockpit. And she realised, amidst her sheer shock, that the motor was turning over, had been all the time.

'Fraser, you *can't* do this!' she began as he cast off the one rope that had been holding the boat to the jetty and put the throttle into reverse.

'Don't make a scene, Saffron,' he murmured, looking over his shoulder as he started to reverse the yacht carefully out. 'Or I'll lock you in the cabin.'

'You'll *what*?'

He looked down at her. 'Isn't that what a good pirate would do?'

Her mouth fell open—something he took advantage of to add, 'Be a good girl and don't talk for a while. Not until I get us out of the marina, anyway.'

'But...but where are we going?'

'Wherever the whim takes me, Saffron.'

'Delia,' she said dazedly as they left the marina

behind and slid into the north arm of the Coomera river. 'Delia agreed to this? Connived with you even?'

'She did.' He was standing at the big stainless-steel wheel with his legs braced as the wash of a power boat rocked them. 'She said to tell you that she's able to take care of everything for a while.'

'I don't believe this.' Her eyes were still stunned, and he smiled slightly as he glanced down at her.

'I would if I were you. You always told me I'd make a good pirate.'

'Fraser,' she whispered, 'don't do this. I can't... take any more.'

'It's strange you should say that, Saffron. Neither, I found, could I.'

'But nothing's changed...'

'Yes, it has. Listen, though, I've got some tricky manoeuvring to do through these channels if we don't want to run aground. Why don't you have a look around?'

It can't be what I hope it is, she told herself as she climbed down into the main cabin. Why am I even agreeing to this suggestion?

What else could you do? she answered herself with irony as she stood at the foot of the companionway and looked around. It was a spacious and comfortable main salon with lovely woodwork and a neat galley. The built-in couches were covered in maroon velour, the carpet was rose-pink and the portholes were genuine polished brass.

She turned and went down another short set of stairs to what turned out to be the aft cabin. A miniature stateroom with a walk-around double bed, it had a masculine flavour—a navy and white fitted and quilted spread, an off-white carpet, more lovely woodwork and brass fittings, all highly polished. But what riveted her attention were the carrier bags on the bed. Elegant bags from Gold Coast shops that she knew well…

She up-ended the first and a yellow bikini slid out with a yellow and white sarong to match. The second yielded some shorts and shirts. The third a lovely summer dress with a long skirt and a halter-neck bodice. Her hands started to shake as she found a package of the cosmetics she used still in their wrappings, a hairbrush, toiletries, even a selection of scrunchies to tie her hair back with…

The last carrier bag revealed underwear and nightwear. All silk or the finest cotton, all beautiful, all a bit more than she could bear.

She swung round precipitately, realised the motor had been cut and heard the anchor chain rattle out. Her eyes widened, and she made a sudden decision. They couldn't be far from Sanctuary Cove although she had no idea why they'd stopped. But there were always plenty of boats on the river, it wasn't that wide and, anyway, there were plenty of sandbanks…

'Sorry,' Fraser said wryly as she appeared at the top of the companionway, 'but we're going to need a bit more tide to get through here— *Saffron*! You idiot…'

But the rest of his words were drowned, literally, as she glanced around swiftly, chose a spot, kicked her shoes off and dived neatly over the side of the *Buccaneer*.

She surfaced, gasping a little, then started to swim

strongly for the nearest bank. She didn't see him dive in or surface—didn't hear anything—so couldn't believe how soon it was that she felt a pair of hands grab her feet then haul her into his arms. Once there, although gasping again and fighting furiously, she couldn't doubt that Fraser Ross was in the grip of a towering rage.

'You blasted, bloody fool—stop it!' he yelled at her. 'You'll get us both drowned.' And, when she still fought, he cursed her again and warned her that he'd give her a clip on the jaw if he had to.

What stopped her was in fact exhaustion, and he swam back to the yacht with her in the classic lifesaver grip. 'Up,' he said grimly, holding onto the stainless-steel ladder that ran down the transom.

'Fraser...' she panted. 'I...'

'Up,' he repeated murderously, and gave her a less than gentle shove in an upward direction.

She crawled up the ladder to collapse on the deck when she got there. But she didn't get much respite because he jerked her to her feet, slung her over his shoulder and took her down the companionway like a rag doll.

'Don't you ever—' he set her on her feet '—do anything like that again. I never thought you were a fool, Saffron Shaw, but I'm beginning to wonder!' He shook her.

Water streamed off both of them. His dark hair was plastered to his head, his yellow T-shirt was mud-stained.

Saffron plucked a slimy reed off the front of her blouse and her teeth chattered, although not so much from cold. 'We're m-making a mess on the c-carpet.'

'To hell with the carpet.' He shook her again.

'That's...that's very pirate-like, Fraser, but would you mind not doing it again? You're giving me a headache.'

'No pirate in his right mind would want to be saddled with *you*.'

'I could have told you that.' She wiped her face with her hands, brushing her hair back at the same time, then grimacing at the shower of drips she created. 'What...what are you *doing*?'

'Ripping your blouse off,' he said through his teeth as buttons sprayed everywhere. 'You've just reactivated my buccaneer tendencies, Saffron—and don't look like that. You surely didn't think I'd let you swim away to heaven knows what fate in the Coomera river? Here.' He pulled the blouse off her, opened a cupboard and handed her a towel from it. 'Take your trousers off.'

'If you're suggesting I *asked* for this—' She stopped abruptly, but only because he was taking her trousers off for her. '*I* can do it,' she panted as their hands tangled. 'I'd have been quite safe—'

'Then do it—like hell you would have,' he said shortly, and turned away to get a towel for himself, pulling his T-shirt off at the same time.

It required some contortions to get out of the slim, sopping trousers then she wrapped the towel around her sarong-style and raised her hands to squeeze out her hair.

'Stay there,' he ordered, and disappeared down into the aft cabin.

Saffron took a distraught breath but he was back before she could make any decisions. Back wearing dry shorts and rubbing his hair. 'Now,' he said, looming over her.

'Fraser, I'm sorry about that.' She rushed into speech. 'But I'm not built to be mistress material either. Please; I thought you understood that,' she said barely audibly as their gazes clashed.

'Who said anything about mistresses?'

'That's what I assumed you had in mind...' Her lips trembled. 'I couldn't do it.'

He dropped his towel and put his hands on her shoulders. 'Would you like to tell me why?'

Her heart sank like a stone and she looked away, but he slid one hand up her neck and tilted her chin towards him with his thumb. 'Saffron?'

Her battered heart started to beat heavily because of the intensity of his dark gaze, the gentle pressure of his thumb on her chin, the proximity of his big body which had been such a haven to her once and had taken her to such a star-shot heaven...

She took a quick little breath and closed her eyes. The truth? Perhaps only the truth would save her any more heartache. Once he knew the truth he would have to let her go, wouldn't he?

Her wet lashes lifted and, although she didn't know it, her green eyes were heartbroken. 'I didn't tell you I was crying as well, did I?'

'Crying?'

'When I bumped into your car. So it wasn't really the rain; I don't think it had much to do with the rain actually. I was crying because there wasn't to be a baby. I don't know why, but I couldn't stop thinking about it. It really came as quite a shock, the way it—' she swallowed '—occupied my thoughts. I...I mean, me, Saffron Shaw, career girl extraordinaire, who had never really stopped to think about children before...'

'You wanted there to be a baby? Ours?'

She nodded and sniffed. 'Strange, isn't it?'

'Not if you love me, no.'

'Yes, well.' She twisted her hands suddenly. 'That's why I'd be no good as your mistress, Fraser, so—'

'*Say* it, Saffron.'

Her eyes widened. 'You want me to say...I love you?'

'Why do you think I did this?' he asked roughly. 'Because I love *you*, Saffron. I can't live without you, and not as a mistress. I need you far more than that. Do you think *I* wasn't pinning my hopes on an un-planned pregnancy to resolve this...this impasse? This crazy situation of whose career was the more important?'

'You...want to marry me?' Saffron whispered, ab-solutely stunned.

'You little fool,' he said, gathering her into his arms and holding her so close that she could feel the way his heart was beating. 'I've never been the same since you danced past in your lovely gown. I never will be the same again—' his voice softened '—my beautiful, tormenting, wildcat wife-to-be.'

'Oh, Fraser,' she gasped, 'when did this happen?'

He stared down at her and his lips twisted. Then he kissed her, picked her up and took her over to one of the maroon settees. 'I told you, when I first saw you.' He sat down and cradled her to him.

For a moment, Saffron thought she might die of joy. Then sanity prevailed and, although she had her hands cupped around his face as she did so, she said, 'But I was sure, right up until the last time we met, that…that *you* were sure it couldn't work.'

'In my ignorance, my stupidity and arrogance,' he said dryly, 'yes. I couldn't see how it could work right up until then. When it dawned on me that I'd cut the last tie, it was an entirely different matter. That's when it also dawned on me that your comment on wiping the slate clean had infuriated me because if there'd been one sign that you were going through the kind of hell I was I'd have asked you to marry me there and then.'

'You told me I looked pale and washed out…'

'And you had a legitimate reason for it,' he countered.

'If only you knew…' She shuddered suddenly and tears spilled over as all sorts of emotions churned up within her, including the memory of that unspoken challenge in the air that last day—which suddenly made sense of *this*. 'I so nearly told you I'd be anything you wanted me to be because I could only ever love you, but, you see, I just knew I couldn't be a mistress.'

'Hush,' he said, so gently, she smiled through her tears.

'You often say that to me,' she murmured.

'Because you're such an all-or-nothing person. Do you believe me now, Saffron? I can tell you more if you like. I can tell you, for example, how right you were about me.' He paused and laid his head back. 'How I had decided—clinically, I guess—that it might be time to start looking for the right kind of wife.'

Saffron winced a little. 'I may not make a very conventional kind of wife.'

He lifted his head and looked down at her with such wicked amusement as well as so much love in his eyes, she could barely breathe, she found.

'Who wants a conventional wife when they can have all this?' he said softly. 'Someone I adore, someone who never bores me, someone who—unless I'm around to make love to her and look after her—is on my mind so that I can't concentrate on anything else.'

'Really?'

'Cross my heart. You accused me once of being a buccaneer, Saffron, but do you honestly believe I make a habit of this?'

'Kidnapping girls?' she suggested gravely.

'Precisely,' he agreed. 'Pirating them away—because I was deathly afraid you might not agree to anything else.'

'S-so—' her voice shook a little '—what do you have in mind for me now, Fraser?'

'Sailing you up to the Whitsundays—quite an adventure, I think. Making love to you whenever we feel like it—I know this isn't a galleon but it is well-named.'

She blushed.

He kissed her hair, and went on, 'Living like gypsies for a while, not bothering much about clothes, eating when we feel like it, catching our own fish and lobsters, enjoying the sea and the sun and the moon and the stars. There's music on board, quite a little library. And, when we get there, instead of Delia putting our house in order, we could do it ourselves. Dad and Delia can be our first guests.'

'That's fantastic...'

'One thing I didn't mention is getting married along the way. How about Mooloolaba? It's our next stop anyway.'

'I don't know what to say...'

'That has to be a first.' He looked down at her wryly.

'That doesn't mean to say I don't know what to do.' She sat up and unwound the towel, revealing her drenched bra and briefs. 'I know I claimed I *didn't* make a habit of this, but...' She stopped and sighed, and suddenly buried her head against his shoulder. 'I've missed you so much, Fraser.'

'My darling Saffron,' he said in a different voice, 'so have I. Were you planning to seduce me?'

'Yes,' she whispered. 'But I'd much rather you did the honours this time.'

Their lovemaking in the aft cabin was like no other. It was like the tide around them, a tide of passion, rising to a crescendo and a fulfilment that saw Saffron dewy with sweat afterwards, and languorous with absolute love.

'All right?' he said gently as he smoothed her heavy, damp hair back.

She hid her face for a moment as her body trembled finely.

But he made her look at him. 'You don't have to hide anything any more, sweetheart.'

'I'm afraid I...go a bit overboard for you,' she confessed shakenly.

He glanced along the twisted grace of her delicate body and said not quite evenly, 'If you think I mind, it's one of the things I love about you. If you think I'm not overboard, sunk, lost over you, you're mistaken.' He took her in his arms.

'I love you so much, Fraser,' she murmured tearfully.

'Hush... You're home, Saffron. I love you.'

'We've missed the tide,' he said later. 'We'll have to spend the night here.'

They were up, it was growing dark and they were side by side on the maroon settee, wearing matching towelling robes and sipping chilled white wine. They were holding hands. It was as if they couldn't stand not to be touching each other, couldn't stand to break the physical contact.

'It doesn't matter, does it?' she said dreamily.

He grinned and kissed the top of her head. 'There's something I wanted to show you.'

'Oh? I don't know if I could stand any more surprises.'

'This one I know you'll love.'

'I could never love anything more than what's just happened to me.'

'Come and see all the same,' he said, but with a certain amount of satisfaction in his voice.

She glanced up at him and he looked rueful. They laughed together. 'All right, lead me to it,' she said a little later.

'It' turned out to be the forward cabin.

'This is incredible,' Saffron said slowly, looking around. It was set up as an office complete with a plain paper fax machine.

'My side, your side.' He gestured.

Saffron advanced to her side. There was a desktop with an angled lamp poised over it, and a padded stool in front of it. There was cartridge paper, pads, pens, coloured felt pens—in fact everything she would need to design interiors. There was also a folder on the desk neatly marked 'Guest house'.

'How...?' She turned to stare at Fraser.

'Delia copied it for me. So, if inspiration does happen to strike when we're in a calm anchorage, it's all there for you. For my part, I've had a satellite telephone installed as well as the fax so I'm instantly available if need be.'

'And you don't mind—?' She stopped abruptly and picked up his wrist to kiss the inside of it as tears of joy trickled onto it.

'How could I mind? I'm as compulsive as you are, my darling.'

'But...'

'Saffron, that's where we went wrong earlier, don't you see?' he said gently, and put his arms around her. 'We thought one of us would have to change. More specifically, career-wise, that it would have to be you. But it doesn't have to be like that if we can both make certain modifications and take full advantage of modern technology; that's all. And now we have each other we might just find that'll be surprisingly easy.'

'I believe you,' she said huskily. 'So you really don't mind if I do *some* work?'

'I really don't mind. By the way, I'm moving.'

She blinked. 'Where? Why?'

'I'm tempted to say it's a case of Mohammed coming to the mountain, but you're so unmountainlike except in spirit,' he said gravely, 'that it's not exactly fitting. I'm buying Dad's house from him——he wants something smaller, anyway.'

'You're coming to Sanctuary Cove?'

'Uh-huh. I hope you approve.'

'You've done all this for me?'

He sat down on the stool and drew her between his legs. 'No, I've done it for me. I told you, I just can't live without you, Saffron. But the last thing I want to do is change you, so——well, I had to do something to improve my credibility, didn't I?' His dark eyes were wry but full of something else too.

Saffron trembled in his arms and said very quietly, 'I have no words to tell you how deeply I feel. Only this.' She undid the sash of her robe so that it fell open.

He gazed at her rose-tipped breasts then buried his face between them, and she clasped her hands around his head and bent to kiss it.

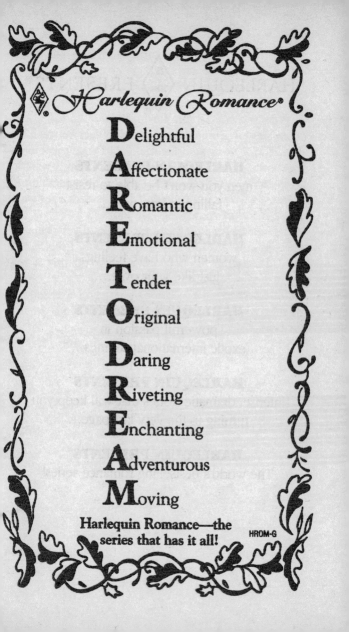

Harlequin Romance®

Delightful
Affectionate
Romantic
Emotional
Tender
Original
Daring
Riveting
Enchanting
Adventurous
Moving

Harlequin Romance—the
series that has it all!

HROM-G

HARLEQUIN PRESENTS

HARLEQUIN PRESENTS
men you won't be able to resist
falling in love with...

HARLEQUIN PRESENTS
women who have feelings
just like your own...

HARLEQUIN PRESENTS
powerful passion in
exotic international settings...

HARLEQUIN PRESENTS
intense, dramatic stories that will keep you
turning to the very last page...

HARLEQUIN PRESENTS
The world's bestselling romance series!

Harlequin® Historical

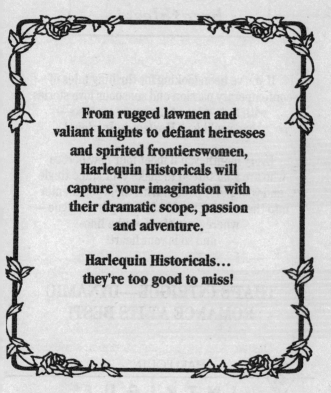

From rugged lawmen and
valiant knights to defiant heiresses
and spirited frontierswomen,
Harlequin Historicals will
capture your imagination with
their dramatic scope, passion
and adventure.

Harlequin Historicals…
they're too good to miss!

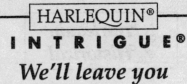

HARLEQUIN®
INTRIGUE®
We'll leave you breathless!

If you've been looking for thrilling tales of
contemporary passion and sensuous love stories
with taut, edge-of-the-seat suspense—
then you'll *love* **Harlequin Intrigue!**

Every month, you'll meet four new heroes
who are guaranteed to make your spine tingle
and your pulse pound. With them you'll enter
into the exciting world of Harlequin Intrigue—
where your life is on the line
and so is your heart!

THAT'S INTRIGUE—DYNAMIC ROMANCE AT ITS BEST!

HARLEQUIN®
INTRIGUE®

LOOK FOR OUR FOUR FABULOUS MEN!

Each month some of today's bestselling authors bring
four new fabulous men to Harlequin American Romance.
Whether they're rebel ranchers, millionaire power brokers
or sexy single dads, they're all gallant princes—and
they're all ready to sweep you into lighthearted fantasies
and contemporary fairy tales where anything is possible
and where all your dreams come true!

You don't even have to make a wish...
Harlequin American Romance will grant your every desire!

Look for Harlequin American Romance
wherever Harlequin books are sold!

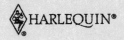

Not The Same Old Story!

Exciting, glamorous romance stories that take readers around the world.

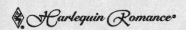
Sparkling, fresh and tender love stories that bring you pure romance.

Bold and adventurous—Temptation is strong women, bad boys, great sex!

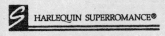
Provocative and realistic stories that celebrate life and love.

Contemporary fairy tales—where anything is possible and where dreams come true.

Heart-stopping, suspenseful adventures that combine the best of romance and mystery.

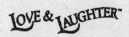
Humorous and romantic stories that capture the lighter side of love.